RATS OF THE HARBOR:
THE COMPLETE CASES OF DIRK AND BAKER

OTHER BOOKS IN THE ARGOSY LIBRARY:

Tarantula Tower: The Adventures of Scarlet and Bradshaw, Volume 4

BY THEODORE ROSCOE

Henry Plays a Hunch: The Complete Tales of Sheriff Henry, Volume 5

W.C. TUTTLE

King of the Dead: The Saga of Monella, Volume 3

FRANK AUBREY

Cave of the Blue Scorpion: The Adventures of Peter the Brazen, Volume 5

LORING BRENT

The Monster of the Lagoon: The Complete Adventures of Singapore Sammy, Volume 3

GEORGE F. WORTS

The Fourteen Points

ARTHUR B. REEVE

War Dragons: The Complete Adventures of Cordie, Soldier of Fortune, Volume 4

W. WIRT

Shark Trail: The Complete Adventures of Bellow Bill Williams, Volume 3

RALPH R. PERRY

Minions of the Shadow

WILLIAM GRAY BEYER

RATS OF THE HARBOR

THE COMPLETE CASES OF DIRK AND BAKER

RAY CUMMINGS

ILLUSTRATED BY

SAMUEL CAHAN

COVER BY

VIRGIL FINLAY

STEEGER BOOKS • 2021

PUBLISHING HISTORY

"Bandits of the Cylinder" originally appeared in the August 29, 1931 issue of *Argosy* magazine (Vol. 223, No. 4). Copyright © 1931 by The Frank A. Munsey Company. Copyright renewed © 1958 and reassigned to Steeger Properties, LLC. All rights reserved.

"The Disappearance of William Roger" originally appeared in the January 2, 1932 issue of *Argosy* magazine (Vol. 226, No. 4). Copyright © 1932 by The Frank A. Munsey Company. Copyright renewed © 1959 and reassigned to Steeger Properties, LLC. All rights reserved.

"Rats of the Harbor" originally appeared in the December 24 & 31, 1932 issues of *Argosy* magazine (Vol. 235, Nos. 1 & 2). Copyright © 1932 by The Frank A. Munsey Company. Copyright renewed © 1960 and reassigned to Steeger Properties, LLC. All rights reserved.

"About the Author" originally appeared in the September 1940 issue of *Fantastic Novels* magazine. Copyright © 1940 Popular Publications, Inc. Copyright renewed © 1967 and reassigned to Steeger Properties, LLC. All rights reserved.

Visit argosymagazine.com for more books like this.

TABLE OF CONTENTS

BANDITS OF THE CYLINDER

Science plays a great part in crime, in the America of 1981, but Franklin Dirk of the secret service finds that nerve and brains are still all-important

CHAPTER I

BLUE RAYS OF DEATH

DIRK AND I both saw the flash—the small blue beam of a ray-gun on a shadowed rise of ground ahead and to the left of us. I shoved on the brakes and slowed down.

"A shot, chief!"

"Yes. Looked like it."

Then we saw three more. They seemed coming from the doorway of a small house set in a grove of trees a few hundred feet back from the traffic viaduct. Some one was standing up there firing into the night.

Dirk leaned over and shouted: "Unfold the wing! We'd better hop up there and find out what's going on."

We were rolling along the viaduct at twenty or thirty miles an hour. It was about 3 a.m., and there chanced to be no cars passing in this segment at the moment. I turned a switch. The wing came out over us, but still I hcld us to thc road.

There were shouts coming from the little hill now—an uproar there.

"Jac, look! Somebody making off!" We saw the blob of a figure running down the hill away from the house. "Lift us!" Dirk added. "Land in there—see what the devil it's all about."

The house was a trifle ahead of us and to the left. I put on the power and raised us off the road. We skimmed over the viaduct parapet and missed the first of the tall elm trees by inches. There was no moon this night. The house on the brow of the hill showed vaguely in the starlight. The shouts up there had suddenly stopped. But we could see the escaping figure slanting down the other side of the hill.

"Land us!" Dirk repeated. "There's an open space—over by that path! Drop us down!"

We seemed to have fallen into some sort of a crime. Franklin Dirk, my chief, was at this time consulting criminologist in government service. We were returning this night in 1981 to our office in Great-New York from a week's vacation in Canada. Under Dirk's vehemence I brought our Bat down with a bump into the soft ground of what seemed to be a flower bed.

The wheels mired in and the up-tilting stern tumbled us out; but we had done that so many times before that we landed safely like cats on out feet.

Dirk had his gun in hand. "There he goes, Jac! Under that line of trees!" Dirk was off on a run. He flung back at me: "Don't shoot him—can't tell what the devil this is. Head him off—over there to the left by the wall."

There was no danger of my shooting any one. My gun was locked up in the car; it would have taken me ten minutes to unpack it.

"Watch yourself," Dirk shouted. "Keep back—go down by the end of the wall!"

I ran that way. The figure had momentarily disappeared. Dirk slipped into a heavy clump of shrubbery. I lost sight of him; then I saw him drawn up cautiously behind the trunk of a tree. The

Jac pinned down the murderous prowler.

stone and concrete wall was a barrier before me. It was twelve or fifteen feet high—too smooth and too high to mount. Our quarry undoubtedly had not climbed over it.

I dropped flat into a little hollow and lay listening. The fugitive had to be near by, for we had seen him come down this slope. Our abrupt arrival had sent him plunging off toward the wall, and when he found he couldn't climb it there was no time to get back past us.

FROM TWO hundred feet to the side of me suddenly came Dirk's voice.

"Hi, there! Stop, or I'll flash you! Stop, I say!"

A man's figure came lunging from a thicket almost directly at me. He had seen Dirk, but not me. Dirk's blue beam flashed into the trees over our heads with its simultaneous little thunderclap.

I rose up as the fellow passed and caught his legs. He came down with a bump; the gun in his hand was knocked away from him.

We rolled in the hollow. I am a pretty solid six-footer; this antagonist felt considerably smaller. He threshed and banged at my face with his fists, but I had him pinned in a moment and was sitting on his chest when Dirk dashed up.

"Good enough, Jac! Lift him up. Watch out for his weapons."

I climbed off him and yanked him to his feet.

"Put your hands out," I told him.

"Search him, Jac," said Dirk.

"I got no weapons," the fellow panted.

"He had a gun, chief. It's on the ground over there."

Dirk picked up the gun. I snapped the steel over our captive's wrists.

"You got no right doin' that," he protested.

"Haven't we?" said Dirk. "That can come later. What were you doing up at that house?"

He was a slim, pale-faced fellow in his early twenties. He stared at his feet sullenly while Dirk searched him. He had no additional weapons. Nothing on him at all that seemed criminal.

From up at the house a man was calling down to us. "You down there—what are you doing?"

"We'll go up," said Dirk. "Come on you. What's your name?"

But our prisoner only stared at us dumbly. We pushed him between us up the slope of the hill toward the house.

"Don't want to talk, eh?" said Dirk.

I laughed. "He's been nipped before, chief. He's busy thinking."

"I wasn't at the house," the fellow said abruptly.

"No?" I retorted. "Where were you running from, and why?"

"I was crossin' the hill. I seen shootin' an' it scared me so I ran."

"That all?" Dirk demanded.

"Yes, that's all. You let me go. I done nothin' you can nip me for."

"We'll see what they say at the house," said Dirk.

IT SEEMED a more or less routine burglary. The house was occupied by a bachelor, one Robert Rance. He was a government employee in the Postal Service—a traffic director of the vacuum tube cylinders in the Yonkers Division. He lived here alone with one manservant named Jelks. The servant had been awake, had heard a noise downstairs. He came softly down just in time to see a man's figure getting out through a broken window oval.

"Was it this fellow?" Dirk demanded.

Jelks could not say. He had rushed to the window, shouting and firing his flash-gun. He had thought he saw two figures, running in different directions down the hill.

"Well," said Dirk, "maybe this is one and the other got away."

"I never was in here," said our prisoner. "I know nothin' about it."

The uproar had awakened Rance. He had rushed down to find that the little strong-box in his lower corridor had been broken into.

We looked the box over now. It seemed quite a small affair. The lock mechanism was melted away by a hydrogen heat-torch.

"Nothing stolen," said Rance. He smiled lugubriously. "Nothing except my last pay—ten pounds of gold leaf. Everything else seems intact. I seldom keep valuables in here anyway. The bank is the best place for them—serves me correctly for keeping that gold leaf here overnight."

Rance was a tall, wiry man of forty-odd, or perhaps older, with black hair gone prematurely gray. He stood before us in dressing gown and slippers.

"Nothing else stolen—Jelks evidently frightened them off." He eyed our prisoner, who stood sullenly staring at the floor. "Who was with you? What is your name, young man? Why break my strong-box? Did you think I had treasure in it? How did you know that gold leaf was here? And what did you do with it?"

"I didn't break it, I tell you. I got no torch—nothin' like that. I wasn't even in here. You can't nip me for crossin' your hill outside."

The interior of the strong-box was littered with Rance's personal papers strewn around it. Old Jelks was on his knees restoring them to order.

"What are you going to do with this fellow?" Rance asked us. "Do you have to hold him?"

"We'll see what Tarrytown says," Dirk decided. "It's their affair, not mine."

I used Rance's audiphone for connection with the local Tarrytown police commander. We shoved our prisoner before the mirror-grid and turned a light on him; but the Tarrytown chief had never seen him before.

"I'll fly a man right over for him," he told us.

"Will you prosecute him?" I asked Rance, as I disconnected.

The postal official shrugged. "What for? A bundle of gold leaf, which has vanished? Ruining my strong-box, if you can prove that he did it?"

Dirk and I left as soon as the local policeman arrived. The prisoner had all the marks of a professional criminal, but his identity was certainly a secret, for that night at least. The tattooed writing of his signature on his forearm said "John Allen," but under the microscope we could see at once that it was a forgery. And his fingertip traceries were all artificially distorted.

"That got done when I was ten years old," the fellow volunteered. "I was workin' in a laundry an' burned them fingers."

"Well," said Dirk, "it's none of our affair, Jac. Come on."

Rance thanked us for what we had done; the local policeman took John Allen away to hold him on general principles and for investigation of suspected submerged identification.

The dawn was at hand when I lifted the Bat out of Rance's flower-bed and fluttered us back to the viaduct. In fifteen minutes we were lolling into the main north entrance of Great-New York.

"Wonder who that fellow was," I said out of a silence.

"I don't know and I don't care," yawned Dirk. "So far as you and I are concerned, that's the end of it."

But it wasn't. It was only the beginning.

CHAPTER II

THE MAN OF A THOUSAND GUISES

AT TWO PAST noon the next day I had had my sleep out and appeared at the office. Dirk was already before his desk. His mirror-grid was illumined and he was in earnest conversation with our big chief, Harrington, at the Washington headquarters. The image of Harrington's red face showed how earnest he was; but his microscopic voice was submerged by the mufflers so that only Dirk could hear it.

As I entered Dirk was saying, "Of course we'll go after it, Harrington... But please say nothing to Tarrytown—absolute secrecy. Yes, send me the Chameleon's latest type-disk." He laughed. "Well, it won't do us much good to see how the Chameleon looked four years ago, but send it anyway."

What could our Tarrytown affair have to do with the Chameleon? I had never seen this famous criminal, but I knew him well by reputation. For ten years he had terrorized the country with every manner of violence. Upon a dozen proved charges he was indicted; and a score more were laid to him and his under-men. But the under-men were few in number, and elusive. The Chameleon himself was more so. Then at last he was caught and sentenced to the extreme penalty of solitary idleness for life. But within three months he escaped. By some trick of disguise he had walked calmly out of the prison. It was so disgraceful an escape that the chagrined officials had never been willing to explain how it really happened.

That was four years ago, and the Chameleon had never been

heard from since—save that every violent crime for which the police could produce no culprit was charged against him.

Dirk snapped me out of my thoughts. He had disconnected from Washington.

"Sit down, Jac. We've got plenty on the schedule now. That little Tarrytown business of early this morning has Washington somewhat heated up. It's about the Chameleon."

"What about him? You're not making out to tell me that was the Chameleon we caught?"

"Don't be witless," Dirk retorted. "The Chameleon is a much taller man. And older. He's a master at submerging identification, but you can't shorten the length of your skeleton—not many inches, anyway. Nor can you lower the blood pressure. Nor soften up brittle arteries. But that fellow we caught is about the next thing to the Chameleon. That's Jimmy Walsh they are holding up there in Tarrytown."

I had not heard of Jimmy Walsh, but Dirk rolled open his desk and laid all the records before me. Walsh had been connected with the Chameleon for several years. He had been the Chameleon's underling in several affairs—but when it came to a court of law, technicalities stopped the proof. Walsh was technically squared with the law now; he had served a short term for forged tattooing and was honorably discharged.

"That's Walsh we caught, certain enough," Dirk went on. "I saw his type half an hour ago—the pictures look just like him and every skeleton measurement is the same."

"What has that to do with us?" I demanded.

Dirk grinned. "Harrington has just assigned us to the job of capturing the Chameleon. Forty pounds of gold leaf as our personal reward if we happen to do it. Want your quarter share, Jac?"

I did indeed.

BUT THERE seemed not much to start on. This Jimmy Walsh, his wife Fanny—a girl not yet twenty, but with a six-year criminal record—and Fanny's older brother, one Jake Pratt, were, according to official belief, the Chameleon's closest and most active underlings. Walsh was now held in Tarrytown, but Fanny and Jake Pratt were at liberty.

"Probably all three of them were involved in this morning's burglary," Dirk said. "The girl and Pratt were outside and sent Jimmy in—and the two outside got away. They could have done that; run down the other side of the hill just as we rolled up."

Breaking into the strong-box of a traffic superintendent of the Postal Service! It suggested some activity of the Chameleon. A projected mail robbery? We thought so.

There was indeed, more than a fancied basis for such a belief, which Dirk now disclosed to me. The Tarrytown police had made a thorough search of the Rance grounds shortly after we left. The stolen gold leaf was still missing. But a heat-torch was found, quite evidently the one with which Jimmy Walsh had broken into the strong-box. And with it was a paper which Dirk now spread before me.

"What he did with the gold leaf is a mystery, Jac. But obviously he had no time to connect with his outside companions. And with us chasing him, he hid the torch and this paper—hid them down by the wall in the shrubbery as we were closing in on him."

The folded paper was a diagram crudely drawn in ink—a plan of the intricate arterial system of postal vacuum tubes as they converged at Switch-pit 22, in the Yonkers Division.

"Seems to show a good many of the secret switching combinations," Dirk commented.

"Walsh purloined this from Rance's strong-box?"

"Looks that way, doesn't it?"

"What does Rance say?"

"He hadn't missed it in the confusion—that litter of papers in his box. It isn't an official document; merely a sketch Rance was making for himself. He's been studying a way of improving the switching facilities in his division. This is just a rough sketch memorandum he had made."

Dirk replaced the diagram in his desk. "Rance has been warned to say nothing of this. No use our theorizing too closely, Jac. The gold leaf may have been what Walsh was really after. Or it may not. To me, it looks like the Chameleon. Something more important than a little routine burglary."

"What are we going to do about it?" I demanded.

"Whatever we do must be absolutely secret," Dirk said. And though our office was insulated against electrical eavesdropping, instinctively he lowered his voice. "I made light of the whole affair. Not a word to any one in Tarrytown that we're on the trail of the Chameleon."

"We're not—yet," I said.

"No, but we will be," Dirk returned. "I've got a premonition, Jac—call it what you like—that this is going to lead us into something. But news travels fast underground. If there's any sign that we're making a move, if any one knows that we're interested in this Jimmy Walsh, the Chameleon will hear of it inevitably and be on his guard."

"What are they doing with Walsh up there?"

"He's locked up awaiting trial for burglarious entry into the home of Robert Rance—which probably won't be proved. And for forged arm-signature, which will doubtless send him to Albany Prison for a year. If we don't pay any attention to Walsh—"

The red incoming message light flashed on Dirk's desk.

"I'll take it, chief." I opened the audiphone.

"Cylinder in mail class AA from Washington for Franklin Dirk now arrived by mail flyer XL at Bennett Field."

"Coming from there by vacuum?"

"Yes. Expected arrival at your office in four minutes. This is advance notification speaking."

"Thanks," I said.

"The type-disk of the Chameleon," said Dirk as I disconnected. "Tell the switch-girl outside that if it's a small enough cylinder have it routed here to our desk."

OUR LITTLE vacuum tube terminal opened with a hiss in the specified four minutes and the small copper cylinder tumbled out.

"This type-disk of the Chameleon was made four years ago," Dirk said as he took out the disk. "Here he is—look him over, Jac."

I dimmed the office lights while Dirk put the disk in the projector. The full-length mirror-grid on the wall glowed presently with the life-size moving image of the Chameleon. He stood there in his knitted prison suit, smiling at us sourly. Across his forehead the superimposed phosphorescent letters of his name showed for a moment—John Carter. Then his voice came from the magnifier.

"I was born in the State of Ohio thirty-two years ago, and my name is John Carter."

He rolled out the official formula with a queer lisp in his voice. And as I stared, his eyes seemed to meet mine. There was irony in his eyes as though he were telling me that he realized I knew that lisp in his voice did not belong there, but how could I prove it. He stood erect, with arms outstretched in the official attitude. Yet there seemed a strange twist to his shoulders, and he held one of them higher than the other.

"I am not guilty."

He said it with a sudden rasp. The lisp was gone. And as though this were a sardonic jest, his whole figure seemed to shrink. His knees bent; his shoulders hunched, with his head thrust forward, and his body twisted so that he seemed a full two feet shorter. A leering, grinning cripple.

I stared fascinated.

"I am not guilty."

The face was suddenly distorted; every muscle in it trained to abnormal mobility. The jaw was crooked; the cheeks raised so that the twisted mouth was set in a snarl; the tip of the nose was raised; and even the eyeballs seemed protruding as they glared at me.

"I am not guilty."

It ended with a croak of eerie laughter; this grinning, horribly sinister little cripple grimly jesting. And then as the type faded, he slowly straightened, shaking off his pseudo-malformation in a fashion gruesome to watch. There was a dumb blankness of expression on his face as the type-disk reached its end, and our mirror went dark.

"Well," said Dirk, "that's how he looked four years ago. And that's his character—proud of his ability."

I DREW a long breath. It seemed as though something menacing had been here with us, and I felt unutterable relief that it was gone.

"He should have been an image actor," I said, "With a talent like that—"

"He was, ten years ago. But he found crime more profitable." Dirk put the type-disk in his desk. "I will ask you, Jac: have you any impression now what the Chameleon really looks like?"

"No. For a fact, I haven't."

"Nor has any one else. After that type-disk was taken they began removing the wax from his face-tissues. His jaw-bone, nose-bridge and cheekbones had been cut down. With the wax gone his thin face looked like a man seventy or eighty."

Dirk smiled at me. "You can't go around melting the cellu-wax out of people's faces and measuring their bones to see if they might be the Chameleon."

But there was one way he could be easily identified. Dirk produced an X-ray photographic print.

"His left leg, Jac. Take a look at this."

In his youth the bullets of an old-fashioned machine gun had smashed away a good portion of the tibia, and a ten-inch segment of the bone had been replaced by a metal plate. The X-ray photograph showed it clearly in the lower front of his left leg.

"He cannot very well falsify that," said Dirk. "And it's conspicuous enough to show on any fluoroscope."

We talked that afternoon until nearly dark. There seemed almost nothing upon which we could make a start. But picking up a trail is often like that. You grope by trial and error until you hit something; and then what to do next is generally fairly obvious.

What we did was to go to the grounds of Rance's place secretly that night, equipped with the regulation police electro-magnetic shadow cloaks, and put the diagram of Switch-pit 22 back where it had been found. If Walsh's wife or brother-in-law had been outside while he committed the burglary, we reasoned that they might come back here now and see if he had been able to hide what he had stolen.

But we waited all night, and nothing happened. At dawn, invisible within our cloaks, we slipped away.

And the next night it was the same. Meanwhile Walsh remained in the Tarrytown jail, and no visitor came to him. His wife, her brother, and the Chameleon himself, if they were concerned in this, were certainly wary.

"We'll have to think of something else," said Dirk. "If Fanny Walsh knew where that paper was hidden, she might try coming to get it."

"We can't very well tell her, can we?" I demanded sarcastically.

But Dirk did not smile. "Not very well. Especially since we don't know where she is, and don't dare even show we're interested. But Walsh might tell her if he knew how to do it secretly."

Dirk's plan for our next move was coming to him while he talked.

"See here, Jac, with a clever disguise and you committing some petty crime, I can get you into Walsh's cell as a full-fledged criminal. You'll have to go easy—I imagine he's sharp as a knife blade. But you could show him how to communicate with the outside world, in case he should want to."

The thing as Dirk explained it seemed feasible, and the next day we tried it.

CHAPTER III

THE HIDDEN MESSAGE

WALSH STARED AT me with interest. "What you in here for?"

His keen gaze gave me a momentary quiver. Would he recognize me? But the cell was fairly dim. What Walsh saw was a ragged, disheveled fellow with a day's growth on a pale face, and bloodshot, watery eyes. One of the most useful talents a detective in government service can have is skill at ventriloquism; and I had no fear that he could recognize my voice. The line of my nose-bridge was temporarily heightened, which changes any face to a surprising degree.

"Me?" I said with a snuffle. "What's it of your business? What I told them nippers is all anybody gets out of me."

Whatever friendliness I could get from Walsh I knew must come from him, not me. For a day I was surly and uncommunicative. Suspicious of him, as though he was trying to worm out of me something that he could tell the nippers to help convict me.

He laughed at that, and let me alone. But it is normal to talk when you are shut up together with the law as a common enemy. Gradually I talked, a rambling tale of drug smuggling and peddling and I think I acted with a fair convincingness that a little cocaine now was what I needed to clear my fogged brain. Walsh also talked a little—lies probably, for I was always conscious that a move from me would have sprung him into wariness.

Then Dirk, with his tall slim figure bent nearly double and a hump on his shoulder, came to visit me. The precaution screen of fine wire mesh was kept between us; but we were allowed to whisper together, with a guard watching. Walsh sat uninterested in the cell corner.

Then Dirk left, and our guard with him.

"My partner," I told Walsh. "Did you see the hump on them shoulders?" I laughed. "He can fool any of these nippers with that hunchback look. He's Ollie Greenberg! What they wouldn't give to know that, eh?"

Which meant nothing to Walsh. But it was a confidence from me, and perhaps it had its effect.

"Nobody comes to see you?" I suggested.

"No."

"What, they don't know you're here? Or maybe you got no friends?"

"Maybe."

"For me, if'n I had a girl—which ain't so—I'd send for her."

It seemed to me that he started. But at my earnest, naïve look he laughed.

"Write her a letter," he said sarcastically, "so the nippers can read it?"

I leaned down over him. "Got a better way than that. I was in wunst, had a forty-pound platinum ingot tucked away in a dump on Staten Island. My partner—this Ollie Greenberg—he was watched so he couldn't get near it. But we got another guy to go—passed him the word secretly."

I could see that Walsh was interested; I hoped he was thinking of his wife Fanny and that diagram which he had hidden on the Rance grounds.

But he only grinned with further sarcasm. "What you do? Write a letter in invisible ink, maybe? Of course the nippers never heard of that!"

"Better'n that. I was locked up. Ollie couldn't be seen talking to the guy who was going after the platinum, and we was in a hurry, so we paged him on the public news-mirrors. Simple, eh? So simple and easy that it worked."

I was trying to persuade Walsh to let Dirk, in the guise of Ollie Greenberg, page Fanny and give her a message.

Walsh said abruptly: "If I had a friend he wouldn't answer no public pagin'. He'd naturally think it was some trick."

We knew this was so with Fanny, for since I had been locked up here Dirk had tried a public personal page-call for "Fanny Walsh." No one had responded. With the hundreds of bulletin mirrors in the metropolitan area she might have seen it and stepped into the nearest cubby to be connected with whoever wanted to talk to her, but she did not.

"No," I told Walsh now. "Nobody with brains would be fooled. But we paged this here friend of ours with a fancy name. Clever, eh? It was a name nobody but us ever called him. See the idea?" I waited to let it sink in. "When he seen it on the page-board he knew it had to be a message from me."

Blank silence was all I got from Walsh, and I dropped it. But the next day when Dirk arrived to visit me again, Walsh suddenly came to life.

"Listen," he whispered. "How about this Greenberg fellow takin' a message out for me?"

My heart leaped. We had it at last.

"I guess he will. A page call?"

"Yeah." He stared into my eyes. "Can we trust him?"

"What's to trust? You ain't going to tell Greenberg where a big bar of platinum is? I wouldn't trust—"

"Heck, no. Listen, you tell him this: 'Page Kitten Claws.' That's a girl, see? She'll know that's from me. If she comes on the audiphone just let Greenberg tell her Jimmy says, 'Paper by the wall in a hurry.'"

We had it! Within two hours the jail commander yanked me out of that cell, and so far as Walsh was concerned, that was the end of me.

"**YOU THINK** she'll answer it?" Dirk demanded.

"Walsh seemed to think so. Nothing to do but wait, is there, chief?"

It was about midnight. We sat in our office in the mid-Manhattan area, waiting to see if any audiphone connections would be made with "Kitten Claws." Over all the great metropolitan district, wherever there was a public name-mirror—at corridor corners of every pedestrian level, at the terminals of all the escalators and lifts, and at vantage points to be viewed by all the passing traffic—under the segment C, the name "Kitten Claws" was glowing for a few seconds at intervals of less than a minute.

It had been there for two hours now without result. One of the mirrors was visible from our office. Through the window oval, across a spider balcony we could see the ten-foot glowing grid set against the opposite wall of the arcade close under the city roof. The roster of names was constantly changing: there chanced now to be only a few under C. "Caw, William." "Celgrade, Frances." "Claws, Kitten."

It winked at me silently. Vanished, then came again. Would she see it somewhere? Would she chance answering it?

My heart leaped as our audiphone call sounded. Dirk was upon it with me at his elbow. He gave audible connection, but not the visible.

I heard the microscopic incoming voice:

"Central Paging Service."

It was our quarry!

"Registered as wanting Kitten Claws," Dirk briefly responded.

The connection clicked. A low contralto voice said:

"I am Kitten Claws. Who wants me?"

She did not give us the visible contact. Was this Fanny Walsh? Neither of us were familiar with her voice and we could not tell.

Dirk said quickly, "I am a friend—you would not know me, but I am Ollie Greenberg. I got a message from Jimmy. To-day I seen him in Tarrytown."

The voice said, "Jimmy who? I don't know any Jimmy."

"Anyway, I give it," Dirk insisted. "Jimmy says, 'Paper by the wall in a hurry.'"

She repeated, "Paper by the wall in a hurry. Is that all?"

"Yes. From Jimmy; you should understand."

The audiphone clicked and went dead. She had disconnected and hurried away.

Dirk hissed for the wave sorter.

"That call I just had from Central Paging Service—what was the location of the talker?"

"One minute, please."

"I can't give you a minute," Dirk protested. "You ought to have the information ready for me—I registered an advance request for it."

"One minute, please."

"Give me Sorter A-4060," Dirk demanded. "Do it quickly."

A-4060 presently gave us the location. "Kitten Claws" had spoken from a cubby in a distant section of the Brooklyn district.

"Thank you," said Dirk. "Get our paraphernalia together, Jac. Let's start away."

IT SEEMED reasonable to assume that Dirk had just been talking to the wife of Jimmy Walsh. She had been, presumably, on the Rance grounds that night of the burglary. She would remember the stone wall; and now she knew that Jimmy had purloined the paper they were after and hidden it by the wall. She would, we both felt, make an effort now to secure that diagram.

"In a hurry," I said. "Walsh added that to his message. Why—"

"Because," said Dirk, "after these several days which have passed, it's perfectly possible that the scheme, whatever it is, matures to-night. The Chameleon wants that diagram to-night! Fanny will go get it—in a hurry, as Jimmy advised. When I gave her the message just now, she repeated it after me. 'Paper by the wall, in a hurry.' Jac, she quite unconsciously stressed those last three words. She'll get there as quickly as she can. She's way off in Brooklyn, but just the same we'd better snap after it if we expect to get there first."

We had our equipment ready in a moment. The Bat was housed on a take-off platform of the city roof almost directly above us. We went up in the lift, caught an escalator niche and were at the platform in three or four minutes.

We were equipped now with the electro-magnetic police shadow cloaks, our flash-guns, microphonic eavesdropping ear-grids and similar devices; and I carried a small fluoroscope for the making of X-ray images out to a range of some fifty or sixty feet. If Fanny came and secured the diagram we hoped to follow her to the Chameleon.

Once on the city roof we found that the night was clear—an almost cloudless starry sky, with no moon. Starting this way openly from our office, it was possible that we would be followed.

"We take no chances of that," Dirk said as we climbed into the Bat. "Have to risk losing a little time and make sure we shake off anybody who's after us."

The traffic starter appeared to clear our send-off.

"Destination Martinique," Dirk told him. "What level can we use to-night?"

"Tail-wind at eighteen thousand," he informed us. "But that fool insect of yours is too small. You'll be annoying to the checkers, coming down for fuel so much."

"That's not for you to worry over," Dirk retorted.

We lifted into the starlight and took the south through lane at eighteen thousand feet. The big craft went by us as though we were standing still. We had only gone a few miles when Dirk put out our lights.

"We'll take a chance on not getting caught at this, eh, Jac?"

We went up as high as the Bat would safely climb, made off to the west, and then dropped. If any one had any ideas of checking our route, we had probably shaken them off.

It was about 1 a.m. when we got the Bat safely hidden on a

dark side road less than a mile from the Rance place. And in ten minutes more, enveloped in our shadow cloaks, we were crouching in the darkness of the thick shrubbery by the stone wall near where the diagram was hidden.

The paper was still there. We turned over the stone under which it was hidden so that the place would be more obvious. Had Fanny come, failed to find it, and gone? We did not think so.

The Rance house was dark and silent. There seemed no one but ourselves prowling the grounds. An occasional aëro passed overhead; and a few vehicles rolled by on the near-by viaduct.

FOR PERHAPS thirty minutes we crouched within our cloaks. The current was silently throbbing through the magnetized fabric. Hoods covered our faces; our hands were black-gloved. At a distance even as close as a few feet light rays striking us would be bent around the aura of the magnetic field created by the cloak current, so that to the eye of the beholder, the background behind us would be visible. Thus, to that beholder we could not be seen. It was far from perfect invisibility, but it served upon all ordinary occasions and here in the starlight we had no fear of detection save that we might make some sound.

Half an hour. Then three-quarters. Were all our calculations wrong? Would no one come in answer to the lure?

Dirk abruptly gripped me. "Look there!"

From down by the viaduct base the figure of a woman with flowing braided hair briefly showed in the starlight as she moved along the edge of the Rance grounds, coming toward us.

"Fanny!" I whispered.

"Yes. Probably."

Then suddenly, from the shadow of a tree farther up the hill, we saw a man's figure lurking. Some one else upon the silent scene. Some one watching, not us, but the oncoming woman.

Dirk's gloved hand touched me. "A man up there. See him? And look down by the viaduct!"

Fanny, if it were she, was not alone. A small winged car rolled up the viaduct and stopped fairly near us. A man's figure climbed from it. Evidently this was the car in which the woman had arrived. The man called softly, and the woman momentarily stopped and turned back.

We were too far away to distinguish the words, but in a moment I had my microphonic eavesdropper connected. The woman and man met at the foot of the Rance grounds. I caught in and heard their greeting.

"Fanny, wait! I'll go with yer."

"You better stay with the car."

"It's all right if we hurry."

"Listen, Jake, don't let's take any chance. Jimmy thought I better do the lookin'. If he'd thought you, he'd have said so."

"To the devil with that."

They headed together for the foot of the wall, leaving their aëro on the viaduct. Fanny, and her brother Jake Pratt! They had not seen the lurking figure up the hill. That figure was still there, shielding himself behind a tree. Who was he?

Dirk whispered, "I don't want to capture Fanny and Jake. Let them get the paper and follow them. We can board their car, hidden in the tail."

They were still two hundred feet from us, coming toward the lower end of the wall, evidently intending to search along it up the hill. We had scuffed up the ground and made the hiding place of the diagram fairly obvious. They would find it. Everything was going as we planned it ought to go, save for this third watching figure; Who was he?

DIRK SUDDENLY whispered, "Jac, creep up on that fellow up there. When you get within fifty feet, shoot the fluoroscope. Just a chance—"

The Chameleon? Could it be? The thought gave me a shock. I had supposed he and Walsh were allies.

Dirk was pushing at me. "Get the X-ray of him. And then get up on the viaduct. I'll meet you there."

I started away boldly through an open patch of starlight, since I was invisible and need only avoid moving the shrubbery, or making a noise. The man up the hill was still standing motionless behind the tree-trunk, but from the angle I was approaching I could see him plainly. I got within two hundred feet. Then one hundred. Behind me Fanny and Jake, undoubtedly unaware that they were observed, had reached the wall and were poking along it.

I had the fluoroscope ready. Seventy feet—still I was a little out of range. The man behind the tree abruptly broke cover and began moving up the hill directly away from me! Had he become aware of my approach? I did not think so. He moved furtively, as though to avoid Fanny and Jake seeing him, but not with undue haste.

I increased my pace. But I came to a line of shrubbery; I had to force through it with caution. The man up the hill gained on me; I lost sight of him once or twice. Then I saw that he was running. And from the point I had now reached a small aëro-car with extended wings was disclosed half hidden by a clump of trees. My quarry ran and leaped into it.

I abandoned all caution. But I was too far away; I had been taken by surprise. I checked my run. I stood, baffled and chagrined while the car with its lone occupant swiftly and silently rose, sailed over me and was gone into the starlight.

I recovered my wits to see that down the hill Fanny and Jake were standing near where we had hidden the paper. They, too, were staring at the disappearing aëro. And then they began a sudden retreat for the viaduct. Dirk was close to them, no doubt. Panic swept me. They would board their car and be gone before I could reach it.

I lunged down the hill at a run. But for all my haste I was too late. Fanny and her brother reached their car. I climbed frantically to the viaduct, but I was a hundred yards down it. The aëro came rolling at me, and the best that I could do was leap aside to avoid being struck. It went past at forty miles or so an hour—too fast for me to dare attempt to board it. I stood flattened against the viaduct parapet. I saw Fanny and Jake seated together in the forward riding pit. The tail-space seemed empty. Was Dirk, shrouded in his invisible cloak, crouching there?

The car lifted as soon as it had passed me. It sailed up from the viaduct, into the starlight, following the direction of the other aëro, which, with its single man occupant, had eluded me on the hill and winged away only a few moments before.

For a minute I stood alone on the viaduct, wondering if Dirk would make his presence known. The Rance house up the hill was still dark and silent. These activities seemed not to have aroused its inmates. I could think of no reason for fearing visibility. I snapped off the current in my cloak, and doffed the hood. Dirk, if he were around here anywhere, would see me now on the viaduct, standing by the parapet rail. The night was still starlit, though now, off by the northern horizon, I noticed a rising bank of black clouds, suggesting a coming thunderstorm.

I stood revealed at the parapet for a moment, but no signal came from Dirk. Then a thought struck me. If he were riding the tail of Fanny's car, he would have realized, just as they were starting, that I was too far up the hill to reach them in time. I moved now along the viaduct to the place where the car had been resting. And there on the pavement was Dirk's message to me—a little crumpled sheet of paper with words he had had time to scribble and drop for me to find.

> JAC:
>
> I am with them. Going to Switch-pit 22 Yonkers—now! Take our Bat and come quickly.
>
> DIRK.

The Bat was nearly a mile away, hidden on a side road. I raised my hood, switched the current into my cloak and went off at a steady jogging run. I found the Bat lying unmolested. But ten minutes or more had passed. Could I get down into the sub-basement of the great city and to the switch-pit in time to help Dirk?

I lifted the Bat from its hiding place and soared aloft, heading southward for the Yonkers district.

CHAPTER IV

TRAPPED IN A PLANE

AS DIRK AFTERWARD agreed, we had miscalculated our actions there by the stone wall of the Rance place. When once I left Dirk and started up the hill, there was no way that he could recall me. For a few moments he lay quiet, watching the oncoming Fanny and her brother. They advanced, seeming quite unaware that any one else was there. From Dirk's angle he could see the figure up by the tree, though they could not.

Fanny and Jake reached the foot of the wall and began searching the ground along its base, moving now directly toward where Dirk was crouching. Presently, with his unaided ears, their low voices were audible. They saw the patch of ground where we had scuffed it, and the overturned stone; and they pounced upon the diagram.

There was a moment when Dirk was wholly absorbed watching Fanny and Jake. They were no more than ten feet from him; he could see and hear them plainly. Jake flashed a little hand torch upon the paper eagerly.

"This is it, Fan!"

"What's it say?"

"Plan of Switch-pit 22, Yonkers. That was the one, wasn't it? That dirty rat, pushin' us down to ten per cent. This'll fix him."

He pored over the paper, but Fanny reached for it.

"Give me," she demanded.

"Leave it alone."

"Jimmy said 'in a hurry.' Maybe that might mean, to-night.

Ain't it in the code there somewhere? The time an' the cylinder. He said—"

"I'm lookin'. But it—"

"Give me," the woman repeated.

"I got it. That dirty rat, this'll fix him."

"To the devil with that, Jake! What time, an' what cylinder number?"

"It's cylinder P-288, leavin' the North-Central Depot at 3.50 a.m. That gets it to Switch-pit 22 at about 3.56. An' it's to-night! Fan, it's less'n an hour from now. Quick as we can get there—I'll be damned! Look up there, Fan!"

They both turned to gaze up the hill, and Dirk turned with them. The man I was chasing was visible as he ran into the open, disappeared into a hollow and a moment later up came his aëro, sailing away to the southward. It astonished Fanny and Jake, and alarmed them. That they knew or guessed who the man was and where he was going was at once apparent to Dirk.

Fanny muttered vehemently: "That's him! I bet that's him! Going to the pit now."

They were passing Dirk, hurrying back to the viaduct.

"Jake, what'll we do?"

"Go there! I'm goin' through with this myself, just like Jimmy planned—the heck with ten per cent. I can handle him. I'll drive a flash through him if he don't like it. You, Fan, you're as good as a man in a fight."

"But, Jake, no killing. You know what—"

They were running now, with Dirk after them. Fanny, in her divided skirt wound tight with leather straps around her legs from the knees down, scaled the viaduct braces like a cat going up a tree. They reached the car and were a moment starting it, during which Dirk was able to climb into the tail-space and scribble me the note. And then they rolled down the viaduct and sailed.

DIRK DID not know what had happened to me, but he very

well guessed. He lay crouched in the little rectangle of space over the tail. The two in the driving pit were only twelve or fifteen feet in advance of him. The pit-lights were out, save for the opalescent glow of the dial-faces. Dirk could see the two figures fairly plainly; Jake was driving, with Fanny wedged beside him. He had handed her the diagram. She folded it away into the pocket of her dark linen-corded jacket; and then sat calmly coiling the braids of her black hair upon her head. And in a moment, when she had finished, Dirk saw a flash-gun ready in her hand.

Behind Dirk, back over the northern horizon, a storm was coming up. There was presently a distant flash of lightning, and a muffled muttering thunder. The two in the driving pit occasionally spoke, but the thrum of the motors made their voices inaudible.

From his position Dirk could see over the side of the tail, and down to the Hudson River shining in the starlight. They were at some ten thousand feet; it was a ribbon of river, edged by the great docks and the spider aëro platforms, banked with beacon lights. And close ahead now were the rising ramparts of Great-New York. A hundred entrances were here as a choice, but no matter which one Jake selected, it was only a matter of minutes now down into the city to the Yonkers district and Switch-pit 22.

Dirk was trying to map out a course of action. He was, perhaps, for a moment inexcusably careless. He was aware of the distant lightning flashes behind him, and suddenly he awoke to what had so unexpectedly occurred. Fanny and Jake had murmured together. They abruptly flung up the aëro's cross-wind vizor. It rose like a curtain between Dirk and them.

Dirk had hardly time to move from his wedged and crouching position, with his current-charged invisible cloak enveloping him and a flash-gun in his gloved hand. He was aware of a sudden dip of the aëro, a half loop-roll, and all the heavens and the outskirts of the metal city beneath swooped as the car rolled and then righted itself.

Beyond a corner of the raised vizor-shield, Dirk saw that Fanny and Jake had jumped for the little safety volplane board which hung clipped under the right forward wing. It flashed to Dirk then what had happened. The lightning flares as a background had made him briefly visible. They had discovered him; feared to chance an exchange of shots at such close range; and they were abandoning the aëro, sending it wrecked to crash with Dirk upon the city ramparts.

It all happened so quickly that Dirk had no more than time to climb unsteadily to his feet. The aëro controls were smashed. The car dived wildly.

Jake cut away the volplane. With its solid little cross-wing spread, it sailed off at a tangent like a soaring bird, with Fanny and Jake crouching in its center. As they left, the girl's arm flung up. A white bundle hurled from her hand, struck Dirk and fell into the tail-pit beside him.

A fabric balloon crescent! This Fanny, whatever her brother's motives, did not herself want Dirk to die. She had flung him the rolled fabric which in the absence of a volplane had saved many a pilot's life. Dirk had no more than time to unroll it and fasten its harness upon his shoulders.

He leaped free of the car into the dizzy whirling mingled earth and sky. Dropped, then was caught as the fabric-crescent opened above him. The car went rolling past him like a broken bird. Far away over the river, he saw the dot of the volplane board as Fanny and Jake maneuvered it to safety upon a mid-level causeway of the Yonkers city entrance.

There was a brief moment when Dirk was conscious that he was falling too swiftly. The crescent fabric above him, never inspected by Jake and perhaps inexpertly rolled into that bundle years before, was still half spilled of its air. Dirk jerked desperately to right it, but could not. He was aware of a great spider platform—the headway of an escalator—rushing up to meet him. Uprushing lights—

There was a tearing, crashing impact. All the world went dark.

HE RECOVERED to find himself lying on the metal grid of the pavement. A ring of curious pedestrians were around him; and a pedestrian-traffic officer was kneeling, applying restoratives.

"I'm all right," Dirk protested weakly. "Get me up. I'm not hurt."

He wondered how much time had passed. Was it too late now for him to get to Switch-pit 22?

"We seen the chute comin' down," said the officer. "Aëro-chute with nothin' hangin' from it."

"I had on an electric cloak, you see," Dirk smiled weakly. "But the crash made me visible, didn't it?"

"Yes. Stand up. Can't you stand? What's the matter with your leg?"

Dirk had thought he was not greatly injured, but now when he tried to stand his left leg gave way.

He clung to the traffic man. "It may be broken, officer. Or the knee twisted. What time is it?"

"Tri-night plus eighteen. Who are you? Were you in that plane?"

Three eighteen a.m. Dirk realized he had been unconscious only a moment or two. A street emergency light suddenly flashed on, bathing them in its actinic glare. And Dirk saw that a near-by metal pole held an American Press News lens. It was illumined. This scene was already flashing throughout the city on the news-mirrors.

"Officer, I'm Dirk, on government criminal investigation service." He fumbled with a secret recess of his jacket and produced his identification check. "Get that lens turned off. I'm in the midst of a case. I don't want—"

A newsgatherer came shoving his way through the ring of staring pedestrians, and held a microphone aloft.

"Get away with that," roared the traffic man. "This is private." He added, "I'll blank that lens." With his flash-gun he shot a bolt through its wires. The lens-eye went dark.

"Thanks," said Dirk. "Officer, I can't walk. But I've got to get to the North-Central Depot of the Postal Cylinder Tubes before three fifty. It isn't far, is it?"

"Quite a ways. I'm takin' yer." The burly officer raised Dirk in his arms. "This post here can get along without me... Here, you, stop that cage! We're going down in a rush."

The newsgatherer halted a down-dropping elevator cage. Dirk was carried into it. They dropped swiftly through all the levels into the city sub-basement where they boarded a single-seated car of the underground monorail and were routed in a rush directly for the Postal Service North-Central Depot.

CHAPTER V

IN THE MAIL PASSAGES

MEANWHILE, KNOWING NOTHING of all this that had happened to Dirk, I landed the Bat on one of the approach platforms of the Yonkers entrance causeway and rolled into the city. The current was off in my cloak now; I had no wish to startle traffic directors by showing them an apparently driverless car. I found presently a place to leave the Bat, on an upper balcony level of Park 80 in the Yonkers district.

A cage took me into the sub-basement. At this hour just before dawn, the subterranean corridors were almost deserted. There were practically no pedestrians; an occasional passing monorail and a few freight-laden vehicles on the central drive-space. These lower shops were all closed now, their glassite windows dark and barricaded.

I moved along the corridor with my cloak over my arm. The time was 3.40 a.m. I was within close walking distance now of Switch-pit 22. I thought that Fanny and Jake, and Dirk a shadow with them, certainly would have reached there by now.

I stepped into an arcade recess which was dark and secluded, away from the dim blue glow of the corridor tube-lights; and with the current in my cloak again making me invisible, I hastened back into the corridor.

One may travel swiftly within an invisible cloak and with a feeling of comparative safety. The extraordinary penalties attached to the use of these police cloaks have made criminals wary of them, and few indeed have fallen into their hands before the rightful wearer could short-circuit them, burning out the intricate wiring. There was little chance that I would encounter and collide with any one else so equipped. I ran freely down the vaulted lane, and the city noises blotted out my footfalls. I slipped into a monorail car whose lights signified it would stop near my destination—and its few passengers were not aware of me.

At 3.48 I was down in the city's lowest cellar level. The great cellar caverns stretched around me, with yellow spots of light eerie in the gloom. The fetid air—for all the city's boasted ventilating system—was so heavy down here that I could see it hanging in layers. Dripping moisture, despite the modern devices which should keep it clear, hung in glistening beads on the low vaulted roof. The drainage pipes and conduits lay on the wet floor like tangled pythons... I saw occasionally groups of repair workers, ghouls prowling in the gloom. Overhead, the transit tunnels were rumbling with trains; and off to the right the Hudson River bed, I knew, was still higher.

I think that it was just about 3.50 a.m. when I plunged into one of the winding little tunnels designated as a lower entrance to Postal Switch-pit 22. And in a moment more the interior of the pit lay before me.

I stood for a time cautiously pressed against the tunnel wall, peering down into the pit whose floor lay a few feet beneath my level. This was one of the smaller of the many converging centers of the arterial system of inter-city postal transportation. Fifty perhaps of the vacuum transit tubes—each tube some three feet in diameter—converged here. The pit was a low-vaulted circular room some sixty feet in diameter, shaped like the interior of two shallow bowls, one inverted upon the other. There was thus a concave floor and a concave ceiling, with a circular mid-line where they connected.

THE PIT, as I saw it now, was dimly blue lit. The banks of tube entrances, each capped by its heavy metal shield, stood like staring dark eyes. In the pit center, upon universal joints, were the four electro-magnetic cranes, which, with uncanny precision, seized upon the arriving cylinders as they slid out of their portes, lifted them, swung them dangling across the room and inserted them in the proper departing tubes for their new destination. The great location board, covered with tiny winking lights showing the location of the on-coming cylinders, stood in a crescent to one side. And near it were the banks of switches and key-levers by which the cranes and the tube-portes were controlled.

There were, I knew, times during the twenty-four hours when traffic here demanded the presence of several switchmen. But I had anticipated only one or two would be in the pit at this hour. And Fanny and Jake and Dirk—

I saw, with my first quick glance, that two men were here. One of them—the switchman, evidently the only one on duty—stood, now at his key-levers. He was operating only one crane and the cylinders were arriving fairly fast for him. One lay waiting in its cradle on the floor—glistening bronze like a huge double-pointed cigar, a little less than three feet in diameter at its bulging middle and nearly ten feet long. Another porte popped open and vomited its cylinder, and the crane lifted the first one and swung it away.

Traffic was proceeding normally. This switchman on duty now I had never seen before; but the man standing beside him I recognized at once. It was Rance, superintendent of this division, in charge of this and several others of the Yonkers pits—Rance, from whom a few nights ago Jimmy Walsh had stolen the diagram and, presumably, ten pounds of Rance's personal gold-leaf funds which had never been heard of since.

Thoughts are insistent things. I had been standing in the little entrance way no more than a few seconds. I recall that it flashed to me that Jake and Fanny and Dirk had not yet arrived. Rance, of course, knew of some treasure cylinder which was traversing the mails at this hour. He knew its number, and that it was to leave the North-Central Depot at 3.50 a.m., arriving here about 3.56. And since his code paper had disappeared he was personally here now to make sure that the cylinder was properly handled.

With extra guards? I saw, under the electric clock dial, the switchman's routine weapon. And then I saw that Rance and his switchman were not alone here. Two other dark-garbed figures crouched behind the location-board. Hiding there, weapons in hand.

I think I had been about to switch off my cloak current and enter the pit, to join Rance and warn him of the menace from Jake and Fanny. But the surprise of seeing the two crouching figures stopped me. I had at first a vague swift idea that they were menacing Rance and the switchman, but instantly I realized that was not so. Rance could easily see them from where he was standing.

But their furtive, tense aspect gave me pause. And over the clank of the crane and the cylinders, the hiss of the vacuums, I still could hear the voices of Rance and his subordinate. What they were saying gave me greater pause; a wonderment; a feeling that what I was seeing here in the pit was not what it seemed to be.

"Three fifty-three," said Rance. He gestured to the clock. "It should have left the North-Central Depot three minutes ago. It'll start presently." He was gazing at the location-board. "A little late, evidently... Keep up with the traffic, Dowling. Don't let 'em collect on you. We don't want the down town inspectors looking our way. Not at this critical moment."

IT SOUNDED queer to me. The words, or the way he said them. It gave me pause. I stepped down to the floor of the pit, but I shrank against its wall, crouched under a safety rail, invisible within my cloak.

Dowling was busy endeavoring to clear the floor of three cylinders before others arrived. Rance, with his tall muscular figure garbed in tight leather trousers and a gray suede jacket, was no more than twenty feet from me. His stern-featured face, with the iron-gray hair above it, was plain in the glow of a ceiling light. He was grimly, sardonically smiling. He added:

"Damned traitors, eh, Dowling? Well, if they dare come here we'll give them a surprise." His glance went to the two crouching figures.

What did that mean? He would not be talking along that line, it seemed to me, unless the lens-eye and the microphone over the location-board—by which headquarters down town could see and listen to what was transpiring here—had been cut off. It gave me a shivery feeling to know that we were entirely isolated from the rest of the world.

In a little arcade opening across the pit a figure suddenly appeared. Jake Pratt. He stood with leveled flash-gun.

"Don't move," he growled at Rance. "You—by the devil, I'll flash you dead if you make a move!"

His weapon was upon Rance. Behind him I saw the determined Fanny standing calm as a man with her gun pointing over Jake's shoulder as he crouched in advance of her.

Rance whirled around. "Oh, so it's you!"

"Put your hands out!"

"They're out and up!" Rance's arms went over his head. "Don't be a fool—don't flash me, Jake."

Fanny's voice shrilled: "You, Dowling, keep away from your gun! An' keep that traffic moving. We don't want any attention brought here at this time."

Jake leaped into the pit, with Fanny after him. But where was Dirk? I expected him to take a part in the scene.

Rance stood motionless, with his arms above his head. "What's the matter with you, Jake? You, Fanny, what's all this play-acting for? We're isolated from down town—don't worry. I'm not taking any chances. That cylinder's coming."

"Damn right!" growled Jake. "Comin', an' what's in it comes to me. You with your damn' ten per cent—"

"So that's your game, is it?"

"Yes—that's our game!" Fanny had snatched the flash-gun from under the clock. Dowling, narrowly watching, went on with his traffic work.

"An' you're a damn' killer," Fanny put in. "Back him over against the wall, Jake. Get him out of the way. Dowling, you—"

She never finished. It seemed that Rance gave some slight signal. From behind the location-board came the hiss of a shot. It caught Jake, drilled him. His own bolt went wild as he flung his arms up and tumbled forward upon his face. A bolt leaped at Fanny, missed her; and instead of firing, she stood for an instant numb with surprise. Then she threw down her weapon. And she flung herself to the floor upon her brother's body, gathering his head in her arms.

"Jake, you're not killed? Jake, speak to me! Oh, Jake! Brother Jake, don't die!"

ALL THIS had happened in less than a minute. I still crouched, invisible, across the room. The cylinder was coming! Dowling momentarily left his traffic and pounced upon the location-board to verify it.

"There she comes! Five minutes late, but she's coming!"

Rance and his two followers ignored the body of Jake and the sobbing Fanny.

"Get ready, lads. We'll have to work fast... Dowling, don't let us get cluttered up. Get rid of those cylinders."

Where was Dirk? I felt suddenly that everything was up to me. But what could I do? A flash from my gun would kill one of these men, but there were four of them. They would end me in a second once I was discovered.

I became aware that I was clutching my little fluoroscope. Almost without conscious thought my finger pressed its lever. The nearly invisible beam swept the switch-pit. It fell upon the figure of Rance. I made it cling to his legs. And as the bones became visible, I saw the familiar break and the little metal plate.

He was the Chameleon!

I had anticipated for those few seconds that Rance must be the Chameleon. But for my life, had I given it sober thought, I would not have flashed on that fluoroscope. Its faint beam in this pit of shifting lights went unnoticed. But the grid in my gloved hand was not invisible. And one of Rance's men saw it.

A bolt came suddenly at me. But upon the wrong side, for it very narrowly missed me, hissed against the metal wall and the shock of its electron-aura numbing all my senses. I recall that I tried to straighten. My senses were whirling; paralyzed nerves made my fingers drop the flash-gun. I took a staggering step upon bending, trembling legs.

And I heard the Chameleon's voice:

"There he is! Grab him!"

The shock of the bolt had disorganized my cloak mechanism. I was visible! The men came leaping upon me and bore me down.

"SO IT'S the little nipper, is it?"

I remained dimly conscious; temporarily paralyzed. The Chameleon stood bending over me. He recognized me from that morning at dawn when with Dirk I had captured Jimmy Walsh.

"The little nipper! Still looking for that ten pounds of gold leaf I said that Walsh stole from me? Is that it? Or are you after bigger things? Where's your partner?"

Where indeed? In all the chaos of my confused senses, I could only think of that. Where was Dirk? Would he blunder into this, even as I had blundered?

One of the men kicked at me. "What'll I do with him, chief? Dead men don't talk. We don't want any live bodies left here when we get out of this. And that damn' woman; two little flashes, now—"

Fanny's voice came drab, half hysterical from where she huddled over the body of her brother.

"That's it! Go on an' drill us both. You, the killer—"

To my fading senses it was all like a distant drama in which I had no part. Movement of grotesque shadows, and voices.

Dowling's voice: "She's coming. Two minutes! Less, maybe, she'll be here."

"Let 'em alone," growled Rance. "Dowling, hold out the next cylinder. We'll put these bodies in it—dead and alive both, why not? And send 'em off."

"And have this nipper tell all about it?" some one protested. "And the damn' woman?"

"The devil," chuckled Rance. "Dowling can wreck them off somewhere in the tube. A little postal traffic accident with dead bodies that won't tell a thing."

I felt myself being rolled aside. The treasure cylinder would be here in a minute.

The voices echoed all around me. I understood it all now. The Chameleon had made his diagram for the information of Walsh and the other men, who were to hold up the "innocent" Director Rance, alibiing him; but he had withheld it from Walsh, Jake and Fanny, deciding to risk doing the holdup himself, when there came an argument over the division of the spoils.

Dowling's voice again: "She'll be here in thirty seconds, boys. Passin' the last light now."

A treasure cylinder, such as very often passes through the mails. It had gold leaf, platinum dust, and negotiable securities in its bags. It was to be diverted now—switched wrongly—to a wrong destination, where in an outlying district other under-men of the Chameleon were waiting to seize its contents and make off in a bandit freight-aëro.

Twenty seconds. The call buzzer from down town Postal Headquarters was vehemently ringing. Rance leaped to it.

"Yes, this is Rance. Yes, everything is all right. Dowling on duty. I'm here with him… Yes, some trouble with the image lens and microphone—that's why we're isolated… Yes, send a repair man—"

He cut off. "Repair man! They'd better send a crew to take our places!"

Dowling's voice: "Here she comes!"

Across the pit a vacuum porte hissed open. The ten-foot treasure cylinder slid out under the crane.

The Chameleon leaped for it, and called triumphantly: "The label's right! This is it! Lift it, Dowling! Tube 1820 for North Jersey division. Get it away!"

I had a brief glimpse of the sleek glistening bronze cylinder as the crane magnet descended upon it. A man was holding Fanny and me; but the Chameleon and the other man were crowding upon the cylinder. Dowling, across the pit at his levers, swung the crane arm down.

Then abruptly the side of the cylinder slid open! There was an instant when I was aware of a peering face from within the cylinder, gauging the scene here in the pit. The Chameleon and his companion were caught wholly by surprise. They leaped backward and leveled their weapons. But too late! From the cylinder came a flash. Then another.

The Chameleon and the man with him toppled and fell as the bolts struck them. The man holding me jumped to his feet, met a flash and fell back inert upon me. Dowling tried to run, but a bolt caught him.

It was over—a second or two of horror. The pit cleared of its gases and flying sparks. Four men of the city police came climbing from the cylinder. The head and shoulders of Dirk showed as he braced himself against its sides.

"Rather too bad to kill instead of capturing them," Dirk was saying. "But you can't risk exchanging bolts in a place like this. And, Jac, when I fell from that aëro, the quickest and surest way I could get help was to be rushed to the North-Central Postal Depot. We intercepted the cylinder—got the treasure out of it and got ourselves in it." He smiled grimly. "That was one sure way to get here without giving warning."

Fanny was still huddled by the body of her brother. Dirk, upon his injured leg, hobbled over to her.

"Fanny, I have you to thank for throwing me that chute. You don't like killing people, do you?"

She gazed up at him dully. “They killed my brother.”

“Yes.”

He bent and touched her glossy black hair. “I’m going to get you the lightest sentence I can,” he said, gently. “When you and Jimmy are freed, why don’t you try living straight for a while?” I have never seen Dirk’s face so gentle. “It’s a lot simpler and safer, Fanny. And I think it’s more your style.”

But she did not answer; she just sat holding her dead brother’s body in her arms.

THE DISAPPEARANCE OF WILLIAM ROGER

City Manager Roger of Great New York vanished on the eve of the 1981 audit—which put it up to detectives Baker and Dirk

"LOOK HERE," SAID Franklin Dirk, "you two had better be frank with me."

"We are," I insisted angrily. It was a new experience for me to be grilled by my own chief, as he and I had often grilled others. I looked at Beth Roger. She sat in the stiff upright chair of Dirk's office with her hands gripping its metal arms. Her dark eyes were fixed on Dirk as she echoed my words.

"It doesn't sound so," Dirk commented grimly. He was pacing the floor of the low metal room, with its dim tube-lights overhead, the audiphones on the desks and the door to the adjoining laboratory closed upon us. The Government Criminologist's office was insufferably hot this evening of June 5th, 1981. The single window was closed. Around us was the roaring city of Great New York. We were in the Mid-Manhattan section—near Street 42—but the clatter of the city reached us here as only a dim blended hum.

Dirk suddenly stopped before Beth. "When did you first know your father had disappeared?"

"Just this afternoon, when it was made public."

The thing was making a tremendous stir. William Roger, City Manager, Chief Executive of Great New York, had inexplicably vanished upon the eve of the annual Federal Audit of his accounts. The whole city was ringing to-night with suspicion of political or private crookedness. There was as yet no police investigation, but Beth and I had at once appealed to Dirk. I was his assistant criminologist. But I was more directly involved in this case because I wanted to marry Beth Roger.

Dirk turned on me now. "Do you realize, Jac, that you can easily be suspected of complicity in this thing?"

"Good Lord, no!" I gasped at him. "But how—"

"If you two don't see that, you're more stupid than I think. Miss Beth, you only knew this afternoon that your father had disappeared? But he's been gone three days!"

"She doesn't live at home," I retorted.

Beth explained, "Four years ago mother died. A year afterward, father married again. With a stepmother as mistress of the house—"

Dirk nodded. "And you didn't get along with your stepmother? Tell me about her. I've heard—but tell me yourself."

"She was Clara Grayley—a television actress. Her people for generations back were circus performers. She and her brother George did acrobatic tricks—tight-rope walking, I think they called it—for a television broadcaster. Then my father married her—"

"How in the devil could you expect Beth to get along with a woman like that?" I interjected. "She's not much older than Beth—"

Dirk halted my impetuous outburst. "Miss Beth, you quarreled with your father and stepmother, and then left home to get a job?"

"I didn't quarrel with father—only with her. But he agreed with me I'd better leave. I visit him and Clara sometimes. Oh, I tried to like her—"

"Her damned brother George lives with them," I broke in. "He won't work—I don't suppose he could do anything anyway but walk tight ropes. He lives with them, sopping along on William Roger's generosity. How do you think Beth feels about that?"

A FAINT smile came to Dirk's thin lips. It was a strange experience having him turn his keen gray eyes upon me, when so often I had seen him flash them at others.

"I understand you don't know any of these people, Jac? Except Roger himself."

"No, and I don't want to."

A black-gloved hand seemed to grab at him.

"Then stop interrupting. Miss Beth, when did you see your father last?"

"About a week ago. I heard, this afternoon, the public reports that he was missing. I audiphoned Clara, and she confessed he's been missing three days. She and her brother—and Peter Clark, too, I think—have been looking for him. She seemed horribly upset—I couldn't get any details. I was so frightened myself, I didn't know what to ask. Then I got hold of Jac, and—"

"And you came to me," Dirk finished. "Quite so. You mentioned Peter Clark. Isn't he a news-gatherer of the American Press Broadcasting Company?"

"Yes," said Beth. "He's a friend of my stepmother's, and so—"

"You want the facts," I exclaimed. "All right—she talks too slow! This Peter Clark was Clara Roger's former lover!"

"Jac!" Beth protested. "You don't know that for a fact."

"I know what you've always told me! Peter Clark wanted to marry this Grayley woman, but William Roger won her."

"Is that true?" Dirk demanded. He lifted his local audiphone sender. "Get me the history of Peter Clark—news-gatherer of American Press Broadcasting," he commanded of our outside office manager. "Particularly his relations, if any, with Clara Roger—when she was Clara Grayley."

He slammed up the instrument and came back at Beth.

"You think this Peter Clark is still in love with your stepmother, don't you?"

"I told you I don't know what to think," she retorted. "Clara always seems devoted to father—"

"I can answer that, chief," I interjected again. "Beth's father is comparatively rich, and Peter Clark is poor. So Clara Roger is not apt to be anything but a devoted wife!"

Dirk thought a moment. "Roger may just be hiding out, as the city thinks," he said finally. "But if he's been abducted—in the hands of criminals—any move I make to find him might bring him into additional danger. The average crook only commits murder when pushed, and I don't want to be the one to do the pushing. You, Miss Beth—did you tell your stepmother you were coming to me?"

"No! No, I didn't!" Her eyes had filled with sudden tears of alarm. She stood up, tall and slim in her gray flowing skirt and gray jacket. Her dark hair was straggling out of the little gray hat and over her forehead. She pushed it back.

I drew her down beside me. "Easy, Beth—take it easy; he'll be all right. We'll find him."

She sat clinging to me.

"Now for you, Jac," Dirk resumed abruptly. "What were your relations with William Roger?"

"I didn't know him very well. Beth introduced me to him. I've seen him two or three times."

"But never at his home?"

"No."

"And then you asked Roger's consent to marry his daughter?"

"I did, and he refused it. Said he preferred her to be of legal age before she decided whom to marry. That meant waiting a year."

"Did you quarrel with him, Jac?"

"No, I did not!"

"If he let Miss Beth marry now," Dirk went on, "her legal dowry from him would be some ten thousand dollars? Is that so?"

"And the same a year from now," I put in. "But Beth and I told him we are willing to waive the dowry."

"And still he refuses the consent! Sounds as if he didn't like you for a son-in-law."

Dirk's tall, thin figure towered over us. "As it happens, you two have a very good reason for wanting William Roger out of the way. Suppose in forty days he is still missing? If you broadcast now a demand for his consent to your marriage—and he doesn't answer that demand in Personal Relations Court—in forty days you'll get his consent by default, and ten thousand as dowry. I don't suppose you and Miss Beth ever thought of that, did you?"

He flung the question at us sarcastically.

"But, chief," I protested, "we never thought of it! I haven't made any broadcast demand! I haven't ordered any!"

"I don't say you have. I'm showing you what an adverse lawyer could fasten on you."

"But if we never even realized—"

As though to give the lie to my words, the audiphone on Dirk's desk buzzed.

"A recent broadcast announcement you ought to hear," said the microphonic voice of our outside office attendant.

It came in a moment, repeated from the Echo Service.

> *"Demand for William Roger's parental consent to the marriage of his daughter is hereby made this June 5th, 1981, 7.32 p.m., to be broadcast by this service at this time daily for three days."*

I sat there frozen with breathless horror, and Beth swayed toward me, clinging to me.

"Jac, did you do this?" she gasped.

"No! Of course I didn't!"

I had not indeed; and I knew that Beth had not. But the public voice was now proclaiming it:

> *"Jac Baker hereby demands of William Roger, parental consent—and dowry of ten thousand gold dollars—"*

The damning broadcast was on the air! And I knew that within an hour the thoughts of the whole city would be turning toward me and Beth, wondering what we had to do with the disappearance of William Roger!

"LOOK THERE," said Dirk. "Every news-mirror in the city is loaded full of it to-night. There's another."

He and I were on our way to Roger's home, by monorail car speeding us north to the Westchester residential section of the city. We had left Beth at the office. The poor girl was prostrated by the shock.

The big news-mirror on the mid-level of Park Circle 20 was in a moment out of sight; but at the Harlem Esplanade there was another, with a crowd of at least a thousand before it. I caught a glimpse of the words:

> Government detective now in the Roger case. Jac Baker broadcasts demand upon Roger for consent to marry his daughter. Startling developments—

Our little single-seat car whirled us around a turn and the mirror was lost behind us.

"That's bad," said Dirk soberly. "We're publicly branded as

being in the case, right from the start, in spite of our desire to act secretly."

"I'm prejudiced, I admit," I said. "I can't reason calmly on this affair. But you can. Do you think Roger is voluntarily hiding out?"

"No," he returned soberly. "I don't. He's no embezzler—I'd trust him with anything."

"Then he's held under duress. By whom? And why? What motive has any one for wanting him out of the way? Won't you discard Beth and me as—"

"Of course, Jac."

"Then who else?"

"I can't imagine," said Dirk. "We may be able to make a guess when we talk to his wife."

But almost at once it became obvious to me that we were going to learn very little from Clara Roger. I had never seen her before, and Dirk introduced me, not by name, but merely as his assistant.

Clara Roger was either a very good actress, or else she really was—as she appeared to be—in total ignorance of her husband's whereabouts and thoroughly frightened for his safety. She received us in the somber-lighted luxurious living room on the upper floor of the residence which occupied a corner of the balconied block of houses, set with a garden of shrubs and flowers on top.

The three-leveled viaduct roared with traffic outside, but the window mufflers held out the noise. The dim room with its ornate padded metal furniture was cool and quiet—the height of modern city luxury. Clara Roger sat in an easy chair and told us, with trembling lips and frightened, tear-filled eyes, that she had not heard from her husband for three days. At about nine o'clock at night he had taken his small aëro-car to fly to his office—and he had never reached there.

She was a woman in her mid-twenties. Inclined now to be plump, with coiled and braided golden hair, mild blue eyes and a rosebud mouth. Without her present agitation undoubtedly she would be pretty. There was a theatrical look which still clung to her in spite of the three years she had been William Roger's wife.

The brother, George Grayley, was with her now. He was an athletic-looking man of some thirty-five, with black hair and a neat black mustache. He hardly spoke for the first ten minutes of Dirk's questioning of Mrs. Roger. Then he said abruptly, "Why the police get mixed in this, I'm damned if I see."

"But we're not the police, Mr. Grayley."

He shrugged. "Ain't it the same thing?"

At this mention of the police, Clara Roger was swept into sudden agitation. "Not the police!" she echoed. "Don't let them interfere!"

I think I have never seen such terror as her eyes held.

Grayley had been staring at me. "Say, by the way, is your name Jac Baker?"

My heart leaped. I had seen Grayley once before, but I did not think he knew me. Roger was not accustomed to discussing Beth's affairs with her stepmother.

"Yes," said Dirk quickly. "This is Jac Baker."

CLARA ROGER and her brother regarded me with new interest. The man laughed. "So this is the young detective Beth thinks she wants to marry? Well, let me tell you a few things... I heard that broadcast demand you and Beth made. It looks pretty queer to me—"

"He did not file that demand," Dirk put in. "We're trying to find out who did, and why. It was clever—too clever."

"So that's why you're in this," said Grayley. "To clear your assistant of complicity?"

Dirk stood up. "Perhaps. But family affairs should be kept out of this. Mr. Roger may be in danger. If professional criminals have abducted him—"

Clara Roger gave a low cry, and on her face was again that look of terror. Dirk gazed keenly at the woman who was seated in her chair, with her gaze on the floor and nervous fingers plucking at her dress. And he suddenly changed his tack.

"What has Peter Clark to do with this?" he demanded abruptly.

Mrs. Roger looked up with terror-stricken gaze. "Nothing," she stammered. "He—he offered to help—that's all."

Grayley strode over and fronted Dirk. He seemed about to add something to her statement. Then his gaze went to his sister, who was obviously upset. With veiled hostility he demanded, "Is this all you need of Mrs. Roger? This is all pretty hard on her." He seemed urging us to leave.

"Yes," said Dirk. "Good night, Mrs. Roger. I thank you."

"Good night," she said faintly; and as we left she was still huddled in her chair, staring at her feet.

Grayley followed us from the room. "Couldn't talk before her. I'm glad enough to have you do anything you can to help us find Roger. You mentioned this bird Clark. I don't want to make any charges, but it wouldn't hurt you to check up on him. That broadcasting racket, for instance." He turned to me. "You didn't order that, Baker?"

"I did not."

"Well—maybe Clark did. Ever think of that? He's in the same line of business—" He seemed wholly sincere now. "It happens I don't like Clark. My sister does—so let her. That's her business."

We paused just inside the front entrance of the house. Grayley lowered his voice. "For two days I've been tryin' to find out if Clark had anything to do with Roger's disappearance. I think I better not explain what motive he could have."

"We know that motive," said Dirk.

"You do? Well, all the better. But she's my sister—you keep her out of it! She's a good wife to Roger, but this fellow Clark—"

He opened the door for us. "That's all I'll say. Guess I've said too much anyway."

He closed the door after us and went back into the house.

WE HEADED across the esplanade and down the escalator steps to the lower monorail entrance. Dirk was pondering our next move. To me, the interview had been unsatisfactory. There seemed no possible way of getting on a tangible trail. But practically every case is like that. Dirk and I had learned that exhaustive theory and deduction don't lead you very far. You find a starting point, which is generally by chance—or by trial and error—and once you get going, one lead nearly always suggests another. But this affair seemed to have no possible starting trail; then it opened and went with a rush.

We had no sooner reached the viaduct than from a shadowed recess of the platform a man accosted us.

"Mr. Dirk?"

"Yes. I am Dirk."

The fellow was dressed in black, with a hat pulled down over his eyes. He edged us into the shadows away from the knot of passengers who were waiting for the car. He added:

"Are you—I suppose you are investigating this Roger affair?"

"I like to see with whom I'm talking," Dirk said, then reached suddenly and jerked the hat from the man's head. "Peter Clark!" he exclaimed.

I had never met Peter Clark, though I had heard a great deal of him from Beth. He was a solidly built fellow of thirty-odd, with sandy hair and pale blue eyes. He was obviously under stress now, furtive and hurried.

"What do you want?" Dirk demanded. "You taking this car? You go ahead."

"No! No, I'm staying here. Let it pass—take the next one."

We let the car pass. Clark was plainly agitated. He cast swift glances about the now empty platform; and down the incline to the near-by front entrance of the Roger place.

"Mr. Dirk, are you—are you engaged to find Roger?"

"Why?" Dirk countered. "Would you like to print it as news? And cast it into the air?"

"No! I'm not here on business. I wanted you to know, if you

mix up in this it may be very dangerous. You don't know what you're plunging into. That's why I wanted to warn you."

Dirk seized him by the coat. "What do you know about this affair?"

"I? Nothing. But the police mustn't get into it. I tell, you there mustn't be any search. Not to-night—it's too dangerous... Stop holding onto me like that! I'm not—"

"Not mixed in this, Clark? But I guess you are. Four years ago, the records show you as being engaged to Clara Grayley."

Clark's jaw dropped. By the vacuum tube light on the platform parapet near us I could see his face go white.

Dirk went on. "She broke that engagement to marry William Roger."

"Well, I—what's that to do with anything? I'm trying to tell you not to mix in this. It might bring—bring death." He cast another swift glance toward Roger's house. "Don't you know there might be an electrical eavesdropper tuned on us even now?"

"There might, indeed," Dirk agreed.

"Where are you going now? To your office?" Clark demanded.

"My business is to ask questions," countered Dirk. "What's it to you?"

"I'm wondering where I can audiphone you later this evening."

"At our office," Dirk returned promptly.

Clark looked relieved. "Here comes your car. If I have anything I'll audiphone you."

He darted into the shadows and was gone. The monorail car came along.

DIRK WHISPERED, "Over by those passengers, Jac! Quick! As if we were going to board it—"

We hastened down the platform, merged into a group of passengers crowding to get on and off, then darted back into a parapet shadow, and reached a side exit.

"Now," murmured Dirk. "Slip down along those shadows.

Clark is around here, watching the Roger house, for some reason of his own. We'll see—"

We gained the lower level of the esplanade, and gazing up to the pedestrian trail of the viaduct we were startled to see Clara Roger emerge from the front door of her home, a trim figure in black and white as she stood for a moment gazing about her.

"This way, Jac! We've got to get up there!"

She seemed about to call a public aëro-car. We would lose her before we got near enough to follow. Dirk made a start for the upward incline, but halted at once and drew me into a shadow under a network of cables. Clark had appeared up there and accosted Mrs. Roger. The two had drawn behind a little light-tower and were standing seemingly in earnest conversation.

"Jac, tune in on them! See what you can do. This accursed noise—"

The traffic was roaring around us. I held the little listening ear of the microphonic eavesdropper before me, cut in the current and tried with my hands to shield the grid from the noise of the scurrying vehicles.

There was nothing at first. With the eargrids in position I was nearly deafened by the traffic noises. Dirk was bent anxiously over me.

I caught Clara Roger's voice, a fragment "—at the bank. But, Peter dear—"

Accursed traffic! And then Clark's voice: "Clara, don't you understand—all that money—"

Accursed traffic!

Dirk gripped me. "They're going! We've got to tail them!"

I bundled up the microphone apparatus and stuffed it in the pocket of my jacket as we darted for the incline. The two above us were momentarily lost to view.

"They signaled a car," Dirk flung back at me. "I'll follow them—you can stay around here and watch the house for Grayley—he may come out."

But when we gained the upper level Clark and the woman

had parted. She was boarding a taxi, a small public aëro-car; and Clark was moving away among the passing pedestrians.

"Try and stay with him, Jac! When you get a chance, send a message to Beth at the office for me. And I'll do the same when I can."

He was gone. I slipped into the crowd and followed Clark. Behind me I saw Dirk pick up another air taxi and roll swiftly down the viaduct after the woman.

I WAS convinced that Clark and Mrs. Roger had not seen Dirk and me. All this vicinity was dim with eerie shifting lights and a confusion of movement. I very nearly lost sight of Clark, as he moved swiftly through the crowd on the pedestrian viaduct.

I followed. Clark did not seem to be aware of me. He walked rapidly, and when he was well away from the Roger home he suddenly stopped at the edge of the traffic and signaled an aëro-car. One drew quickly up to him. He boarded it and rolled away, down the viaduct.

Within ten seconds I was boarding another.

"That red-barred car ahead of us, see it?" I flashed my Federal identification at the pilot. "Ten dollars in gold-leaf for you—if you don't lose that car. Are you fast?"

"Fast?" He meshed in his gears and we leaped into the traffic. "Fast? Say, chief, nothin' flies faster than this little blackbird you're in."

But we had no need of speed. The red and white car ahead of us proceeded in swift but orderly fashion along the viaduct. We were presently in the Fordham District, rolling along the lowest of three levels, with shops and lighted arcades to the sides and a network of pedestrian catwalks crossing overhead. It was a neighborhood business center which at this hour of the evening was a riot of blaring noise.

Clark's car drew to the side, and he leaped out; but, a square behind him, I was out as swiftly as he. A level higher, and farther along, I saw the illumined metal entrance of the Fordham branch of the Bank of Great New York.

I recalled those fragments of conversation between Clark and Clara Roger which I had overheard with the eavesdropper. She had told him: "—at the bank. But, Peter dear—"

And he had said: "—all that money—"

Were they arranging to meet here at the bank? Had Clara Roger come here ahead of Clark? Perhaps she was in the bank now. Then Dirk should be around here.

The various levels and pedestrian walks were crowded with people. I did not see Dirk; I had all I could do not to lose Clark. He went up an escalator, and I paralleled him. On the second level he stood in an angle of the parapet wall. Obviously he was waiting, watching the front entrance to the bank. And fairly near him, with the pedestrian stream flowing between us, I found shelter and waited...

WITHIN THE bank at that moment Clara Roger sat waiting for a draft-check to be honored which she had just presented for payment.

The astounded manager could only gasp, and ask her deferentially, "Do you want this in cash, Mrs. Roger?"

"In gold-leaf certificates, yes."

"But the danger—you can't carry that much money. Let me deliver it—"

"Do what I ask, if you please. And will you hurry?"

She sat waiting; and by a side entrance of the bank Dirk had gained the manager's office. They stood now gazing at the little oblong slip of paper. It was drawn neatly in ink—a demand in favor of Clara Roger for ninety-two thousand gold dollars; and it was signed William Roger.

"It is within fifty dollars of all he has here on deposit," said the manager.

"A forgery?"

"But it isn't, Mr. Dirk. Our graphologist just passed it."

The check was dated four days ago—the day before William Roger vanished. It was now three minutes of the bank's evening closing time—illegal to delay payment longer. They might have chanced some excuse, but with the wife of the city's chief executive the bank did not dare.

"I've got to pay it, Mr. Dirk."

"All right," said Dirk swiftly. "I'll follow her. Send that canceled check to my office at once."

From behind the wicket Dirk watched Clara Roger receive the thin oblong packet of gold-leaf notes. She was pale, but calm. She did not count the money. She placed the packet in a burnished metal hand-case of the sort women carry, smiled her thanks, and turning, left the bank by its front entrance—walking swiftly and plunging into the passing crowd of people.

For Dirk, I think that moment presented a more difficult task than for me. Yet both of us miscarried our attempts. Dirk saw the woman for just a moment outside the bank, and then he lost her in the mob. And a minute or two later, a block away from him, all the levels and the arcade entrances and the overhead catwalks were abruptly illumined in a flash of white light. Dirk, with hundreds of other pedestrians, rushed toward that crime-beacon...

I saw Clara Roger when she emerged from the bank, but I had no knowledge of what had transpired inside. Clark began moving swiftly forward. I could see his bobbing head in the crowd. I waited. The woman was coming toward me. I thought Clark would join her and both of them come my way. But she swerved quickly across to a parallel walk. I lost sight of her. I had miscalculated what would happen. Both of them darted into the crowd as though suddenly anxious to shake off pursuit. It took me so by surprise that I lost sight of them both.

But luck was with me. I saw Clara Roger again within a minute. She was loitering, and suddenly I thought I saw Clark approaching her. If it was he, he had thrown a dark flowing silk cape over his shoulders. He jostled against her, and I thought she handed him something. They were well away from me, but there was a glint as though she had given him a metal case. Then suddenly he was running, and there was the figure of another man close after him. The crowd tightened. There seemed a scuffle. Then a traffic director's alarm siren screamed, and the actinic alarm-light of the street flooded everything with its glare.

But Clark and his pursuer, whom I had no more than vaguely glimpsed with a vague idea it might be Grayley, were gone. Dirk and I met as we were forcing our way into the glare. Clara Roger had seemed to try to escape; but she was recognized and deferentially stopped by the traffic man. He forced back the crowd and called an aëro-car for her. I saw, and so did Dirk, that she was no longer carrying the metal hand bag. The money, Dirk gasped, was gone! The halted traffic gave her car free space. It rolled forward, took the air, skimmed perilously between two lateral catwalks and sailed into the starlight...

"**MORE TANGIBLE** a lead? I should say it is, Jac!"

"She and Clark! Ninety-two thousand of your father's money, Beth! What have you got to say to that?"

We were back at the office, where Beth had been waiting anxiously for our return.

"But I don't understand—" she gasped.

"You don't? Well, it isn't very complicated. Clark and your damned stepmother—"

"Don't theorize," Dirk broke in sharply. "This is no time for theory. If that check shows what I think it will show—"

Beth gripped him, white-faced, with blazing eyes. "You mean to say my father wrote a check three or four days ago for ninety-two thousand dollars and Clara cashed it and gave it to Clark?"

"That's what the date is on the check. That's what I want to find out—when he wrote it. If it's when I think it was... Ah, here's the check—"

The small cylinder came tumbling onto Dirk's desk from the vacuum tube. Beth sat in a chair, forcing herself to calmness, watching while Dirk opened the cylinder and pounced upon the canceled check which the bank had mailed us.

"Miss Beth, while I work on this check, you try and find out if Mrs. Roger is at home. I suppose she is. Don't talk to her—just make sure she is there. Call the maid, and then disconnect... And you, Jac, call our chief in Washington. He won't be at his office—at his residence, try him there. Say I want Federal permission to force questions on the City Manager's wife under oath. Explain—and I'll talk to him if he wants it. Hurry up, you two!"

Dirk rushed into his laboratory with the check. In ten minutes he was back, check in hand. I could see at once by the expression on his face that he had learned something definite—and startling.

"What did they say?" he demanded of us.

"Clara is at home," said Beth. "Vance, the maid, said she was ill and preferred not to speak with me."

"Good enough! And you, Jac?"

"I got the chief. But not the permission. He says he'll have to look further into the matter. To put Mrs. Roger on oath—that's too drastic."

"Oh, is it? Well, he'll give me the permission quickly enough! That check she just cashed was written by her husband—not four days ago, before he vanished, but to-day! I've measured the oxidation-rate of the ink. Roger wrote it this afternoon, or at the earliest this morning. Get me the chief in Washington... Don't look like that, Miss Beth! It doesn't necessarily mean that harm has come to your father. But it does mean that he's probably being held a prisoner somewhere. He wrote the check to-day—was forced to write it, I'm convinced."

That meant that Mrs. Roger was in communication with her husband, and he wrote the draft to pay her all his available cash. But did he do it voluntarily? The sinister aspect of the thing came like a light in darkness. I could imagine that Clark had hired professional criminals to abduct Roger. The Federal Audit was a good excuse for his disappearance. And some one—Clark probably—had instigated the broadcast demand for parental consent, in order to throw suspicion upon Beth and me. To save himself from death Roger had written the check. And now, would Roger be murdered—and Clara Roger and her lover be left free to enjoy the money?

Dirk finished with Washington. Then he sent out a general order over the New York district for the arrest of Clark. And following that he put through an imperative audiphone call for Mrs. Roger. He sat gripping the instrument, his thin face grim with the intensity of his emotion.

"Are you there? I want Mrs. Roger."

The maid's voice said, "She will give no connection."

"Oh, yes, she will. I have Federal authority. Contempt of court if she doesn't. Tell her that."

He got her in a moment.

"What is it you want?" she demanded.

"This is Franklin Dirk. I have orders to put you on oath. Give me visual connection, please. I must see you, Mrs. Roger."

OUR MIRROR-GRID lighted. Beth and I leaned over Dirk's shoulder. The image showed Clara Roger's pale, harassed face, with the grid on her dressing table showing Dirk and me.

"I accept the oath," she said quietly. "What is it you want to ask me?"

He struck her with it: "I want to know where Peter Clark went half an hour ago when you gave him that money."

We saw the blood drain from her face and lips and terror leap into her eyes. I thought she would faint, but she clung to her chair.

"Why, I—I did not, I don't know—"

"You're lying, Mrs. Roger. On oath, before witnesses. Where did Clark go?"

"I don't know," she said faintly.

"Nor where your husband is held?"

"No."

If it were possible for a greater intensity of terror to surge into her eyes, it came there now.

"Your husband—you know he was abducted by professional criminals?"

"Yes," she admitted frankly. And beside me I heard Beth gasp with horror. Dirk's swift, menacing voice went relentlessly on.

"You know that your husband is a prisoner, somewhere near here—and he wrote that check to-day—was forced to write it?"

"Yes. Oh, if you can—"

"Not murdered yet, is he?"

It made Beth clutch at me. On the mirror-grid I saw that Clara Roger's white lips were trying to stammer something, but the words would not come.

"Didn't Clark let you know where your husband is?" Dirk insisted.

"You—you—"

We saw her fall, and saw the maid rush forward to her. Our mirror went dark as the connections broke. And at once the instrument buzzed with an incoming call. The mirror lighted again. We saw the inside of a little public booth—a man's head and shoulders and his face gazing at us. It was Clark! I leaped instantly to trace the call, while Dirk kept him busy.

"Mr. Dirk? I tried to get you, but you were busy. I want you—I want you to come to me."

"Why, hello, Clark." Dirk forced himself to a sudden calmness, "What is it? I've been waiting for your call."

"I want you to come. I think I've found—I don't dare—"

His voice was breathless; his face held a mixture of eagerness and terror. "It's got to be now. There's no time—" He was almost incoherent. Then out of it emerged a meeting place for him and us. He named it—a lower ramp in the east side section of Manhattan near the water front.

"Will you come there?"

I saw on our image mirror that behind Clark in the booth a

black-gloved arm and hand appeared. Beth murmured tensely into my ear: "What is that? What—"

But I had no time to answer. The black-gloved hand was behind Clark's shoulder and he was not aware of it. Then the hand touched him. He gasped, and whirled.

"What is it?" Dirk demanded.

Clark came back to the instrument. His voice sounded strange. "Nothing… Some one must have thought the booth was empty. Bumped into me, but he's gone… Will you come at once?"

"We'll come."

Dirk flung off the connection and leaped to his feet. "No time now, Jac—you heard what he said. Get our flash-guns. Here, this one is yours. And your microphone—you've got it? The police will comb that section around the visiphone booth, but I doubt if they'll catch him. Come on—I suppose the monorail will be quickest—it will drop us near the river… Miss Beth, you'll have to wait here."

"Jac, dear—"

But I could not stop to talk to her; there was the equipment to get ready.

Dirk stopped suddenly before her, and put his hands on her slim shoulders. "Miss Beth, I know that just waiting, doing nothing, is the hardest thing of all. But very often it's the woman's part. If you're going to be the wife of a detective—" He smiled gently. "Now is the time to get used to it."

And she bravely answered his smile. I think I never loved Beth so dearly as at that moment while she stood in the center of the office bravely smiling and gazing after us as we rushed out.

"BUT IF it's an ambush," I suggested, as we hurried from the office and headed for the lift-car which would drop us to the city's ground-level corridor. "If it's a lure to get us—Clark knows we're after him—"

"We'll chance it—with caution. Jac, whatever you think we know about this affair—I'm beginning to think other things."

And so was I. Clark's attitude—and Clara Roger's—did not ring true to our appraisal of them as kidnapers. The monorail whirled us into the city slums—a dark and gloomy metal shambles as unlike the Westchester residential area as the poles of the earth. It was now nearly midnight. We left the monorail and on the ground level followed the dark city street toward the East River water front.

Rivington Ramp 80 was a small balconied circle where half a dozen disreputable streets and alleys converged. The dwelling houses, most of them ancient ramshackle brick and stone, went up no more than a dozen stories, with rusted iron balconies, and a few of the more modern catwalks dangling overhead. There was hardly a vehicle here—all were high up on the near-by viaducts leading to the Brooklyn river bridges. It was like a glimpse into the shambles of the past—these water front streets. All the criminals of the city congregated here, and the rest of the city was glad enough to have it so. There should have been a patrol officer at his post on Ramp 80, but he had not bothered to stay on duty.

There were a few pedestrians, and noise enough from the public drink shops, and a dance palace near-by. Dirk and I moved around the edge of the ramp. There was no sign of Clark. We came to the side street he had mentioned. It was no more than an alley—a dark gash in one of the buildings. We slid into it—a place of almost fetid blackness. Suddenly I stumbled upon something. A man, lying on the alley floor. Under Dirk's tiny flash light beam we saw that it was the body of Clark!

We bent over him, and he was not dead. But dying, there could be no doubt of that. His roving eyes recognized us. His twitching hand tried to reach for us.

"You came? I was afraid you wouldn't. I traced them—at last—"

Dirk raised his head. "But, Clark—"

"I'm finished. They've done me in. It's—poison, I guess. There in the booth when I called you—"

He clutched at his throat. On his neck I saw a little spot of red where it seemed that a needle had pricked.

His eyes were glazing. "You—I guess you've still got time. It's—they're under the old dock at the end of the street. Or near there. It wasn't more than ten minutes ago."

"Who?" Dirk demanded. "Roger? Have they got him there?"

"Yes. Roger—if they haven't—killed him yet. I was afraid—you or the police investigating—that would have meant death for him. Hurry—"

My mind flung back to that scene outside the bank. The man in the cloak who had been given the money by Mrs. Roger was not Clark. It was Clark who had chased the other man…

Dirk was saying gently, "We mistook you completely, Clark."

"Yes. I suppose—" His face and his tongue were choked with stagnant blood. "Yes. I—it doesn't matter. I don't want Roger to get murdered. She—loves him. She wouldn't—"

His hand tried to reach for Dirk. "She didn't dare tell me much. I did what I—could to help. I'm finished—"

His thickened tongue caught between his lips. He murmured, "She'll—know—I did my best—for her and—her husband—"

He twitched, shuddered, and the light went out of his staring eyes…

"GET OUT your microphone," Dirk whispered. "What a place! Try listening—it may help—if there's any one lurking around down in here—"

It was like a broken rabbit warren. The ancient dock loomed above us. And far higher, and to one side, one of the great bridges glowed with its dotted rows of lights, and the light of its swiftly passing vehicles. The river—as though it were subterranean with all the lattice of structures over it—flowed dark and sullen some thirty feet beneath us. It was of no use now. The city had overgrown it.

Broken wooden rooms and cubbies and platforms were here among the piers under the crumbling dock, relic of a bygone age. From the overhead dock there had been a catwalk to a neighboring structure a hundred feet away. But it was broken now, dangling so that there was only a single cable stretched across the intervening water.

The place was black where we crouched under the dock. I tuned in the sound magnifier. And at once caught the murmur of men's voices.

"Overhead," I whispered. "Some one up inside the dock. Can we get up there?"

It seemed so. We clambered cautiously along rotting planks to where an old stairway led upward. And presently we were in the broken dock.

Dirk clutched at me. "Over there!" I barely heard his whisper. "That light—when you fire, Jac—it's to kill—take no chances on that."

The black tumble-down interior seemed thronged with ghosts of the past. There was a broken interior boarded enclosure and from its window a little light was straggling. And over the distant murmur of traffic noises we could hear now the near-by voices of men…

I caught just a brief glimpse of the interior of that little wooden room as we crept up to its window. The portly, middle-aged William Roger was lying bound and gagged on the littered floor. Two men were kneeling, fastening weights of iron to his arms and legs—men black-garbed and hooded. A third man, wholly enveloped in black and with hood drawn close over his face, was across the room, near where another window looked out upon the river.

That third man discovered us. He leaped and Dirk's bolt missed him. The two men upon Roger jumped erect; but before they could draw their weapons my bolt caught one, and Dirk's hit the other. They crumpled and fell upon Roger, who struggled and twisted beneath their bodies.

The third man went through the window. My bolt struck the casement, shredded it and set it on fire. But I missed the man. His black-gloved fingers clung for an instant, and then he dropped.

"Inside!" Dirk shouted. "He didn't fall far!"

We gained the room, went across it. Beneath the outer window, ten feet down, was a line of planks. The hooded figure had dropped to them. And the end of that broken catwalk was there, its single remaining cable fastened there. The hooded figure was on the cable, running along it out over the dark river.

I fired, but miscalculated the shadowy swaying form. The man's arms were outstretched to balance himself, and he ran like a monkey. I fired again, but he was out of range. He kept on going.

He reached the other dock, ran back along it, jumped to a little connecting bridge-walk; and in a moment we saw the tiny blob of him at the foot of an escalator leading up to the main bridge artery over the river to Brooklyn. We saw him reach the pedestrian throng up there and vanish.

ROGER WAS unharmed, though in a few minutes more they would have dropped him into the sullen river. The two men we had killed were professional criminals, with a persistent police and prison record—the sort of men any one with the price may hire to do murder.

And we found the price of this affair on them—ten thousand dollars each, of William Roger's money. The rest of it was gone—with that third man, doubtless.

Roger did not know who the fellow was. He had always been masked; and he had never spoken, save in a whisper. But it was obvious that he was the man who had hired the other two; who had taken Roger's check, and returned just a few minutes ago with the cash.

And seeing what we had seen of his escape across that single cable strand over the water, we could not fail to guess who he must be. A man with the skill to perform such an unusual feat;

the man who for a television broadcaster had done acrobatic tricks walking tight ropes for the delight of a television audience...

I bent down over Roger where he was sitting on the floor chafing his arms and legs, which were numb.

"You're not hurt?" I asked. "It was a close nip—"

"You, Jac? I hadn't thought I would be thanking you—after that last little argument we had—"

He reached and gripped my hand. He was white and shaken from his experience. He leaned back weakly on one elbow.

"Have Clara and Beth been frightened over me? Where are they? Can't you audiphone them now? Relieve their anxiety—"

It was the thought in my mind, too.

THERE WAS nothing wrong with William Roger's accounts, when the Federal Audits were held that next morning. In the afternoon Roger and Beth came secretly to our office. Dirk had invited Grayley to come for a little private conversation, and he acquiesced readily. When he entered, Beth and her father were hidden as witnesses, and hidden instruments gave sight and sound connection with Headquarters.

Only Dirk and myself were in evidence as Grayley jauntily entered. He was smilingly self-confident.

"Well," he greeted us, "I suppose you've got a battery of instruments to record everything I say. Go ahead—I haven't a thing to conceal."

"You got away from us last night with very great dexterity," Dirk began crisply. "I never realized before what possible use such skill could be to its possessor."

Grayley raised his black brows and laughed. "I heard about that fellow running over a cable. Say, if you think I can walk that cable, you put a net under it and I'll prove how easy I can fall off."

"Quite so," smiled Dirk. "Falling off ought to be equally easy. Sit down. I want to talk with you. We were all at Roger's home by eleven o'clock last night. Where were you?"

"Me? I was playing cards with some friends. I've got a couple of them to prove it, if you want—"

"It won't be necessary. Sit down, Grayley. Hand me your hat. I want a serious talk with you."

My heart was pounding as I came forward with a glass microscope slide, and I saw Grayley's hand go out with his hat as Dirk reached for it. I stumbled on the floor rug. I think I did it naturally—Dirk and I had practiced this for an hour past. And as I staggered, my hand with the microscope slide came down sharply and struck Grayley's wrist.

"Oh—I'm sorry—" I stammered.

Simultaneously Dirk leaped to his feet.

"Jac, you fool! Clumsy fool! Are you hurt, Grayley?"

"No. Not much."

Then Dirk saw the glass slide in my hand and the blood welling out on Grayley's wrist.

"Jac! Good God, is that what you cut him with? Don't you know that's a culture of Clark's blood—and I'm trying to find out what poison killed—"

There was just an instant when Grayley stood staring stupidly at the jagged cut near the base of his thumb. Then terror swept him. A wild panic of terror.

"That? Clark's blood! That—" His voice rose into a scream. "Get me a physician. You damn fools, don't stand there staring like that! Clark's blood—in me! Why, that's death! That's curare that killed Clark! It's death to me now! Get me a physician."

THAT WAS the end of it. During those minutes while Grayley was waiting for the physician (with the deadly poison, so he thought, circulating in his blood) he yielded to Dirk's pounding and made a full confession. He told us where he had hidden the money, and there we subsequently found it. He had hired the two professional criminals to abduct Roger, and told his sister that her husband was being held for ransom. He told her that the abductors had communicated with him and demanded the money of him. And he had promised it, and persuaded his sister that a word or look which brought the police into the search would cause her husband's death. Then Clark had dabbled in it, and Grayley killed him.

Grayley had slipped out of the house just after Clark finished talking to us on the monorail platform. He had met his sister outside the bank, and gotten the money from her as they had arranged. And he had bribed an under-official of the broadcast service to fake that demand from Jac Baker.

Had the scheme been successful, Mrs. Roger would always have believed that the ransom was paid by her brother, and that in spite of it her husband had been murdered.

His confession was hysterically poured out, mingled with wild demands for a physician. When it was over Dirk put him in police custody and sent him from the office with scant ceremony, leaving the officials to tell him he needed a lawyer, not a physician.

In our private office the smiling William Roger faced Beth and me. He took us each by a hand.

"Poor Clark! I never liked him—if I had known what was really in his heart for Clara and me! And you, Beth dear—don't you think you and Clara will be better friends now?"

"Oh, I do! I do, father."

"And you—you persistent young cub—" There was a gleam of quizzical humor in his gray eyes as he turned to me. "I was prejudiced against having a detective for a son-in-law, but I discovered last night that a detective is sometimes a very handy person to have around."

RATS OF THE HARBOR

With undersea pirates threatening the commerce of Great New York in 1982, Government Operatives Franklin Dirk and Jac Baker began a secret and dangerous mission

CHAPTER I

NEW YORK—1982

DIRK SUDDENLY GRIPPED me.

"Don't move, Jac! Somebody else out here is watching the house. See him over there?"

We crouched into the shadows of the pedestrian parapet-rail. It was about nine o'clock in the evening late August, 1982. The house across the small viaduct was a disreputable affair; four stories of brick and stone, with an old-fashioned flight of steps leading up to the main entrance. There was a dim glow of light behind the entrance panel, but the other front windows were dark, except one on the second story. It was a bedroom; the shade had been up a moment before, disclosing the corner of a metal bedstead. Then a woman pulled down the blind; the tube light of the room threw a grotesque shadow of her against the blind, and then she moved back.

Dirk and I had been about to leave; we were not sure if this was the house in which we were interested; it might be one down the viaduct in the next segment. And then Dirk had noticed that some one else besides ourselves evidently was watching this place. We drew down under the parapet.

"See him, Jac?"

I thought I did. It was the dark shape of a man lurking on the same side of the viaduct with us, but about a hundred feet farther along. I moved a little, in spite of Dirk's cautioning hand, until I could see him more plainly. He was flattened back into

Dirk chanced a shot as his quarry gained the roof.

an angle of the rail, staring up at that lighted window, as we had been staring.

Dirk crept along and joined me.

"He hasn't seen us."

"No. Guess not; he's watching the window."

"Easy! Don't talk so loud! He might have an electro-listener."

We waited. My attention went again to the house. All we knew of it was that somewhere in this east waterfront section of Great-New York was a lodging house kept by a Spaniard, where a certain criminal in whose movements we were interested was said to be visiting a young woman. Information from underground criminal sources is generally unreliable, and nearly always vague. In this section of mid-lower Manhattan, a generation before my time, there had been largely a Jewish population. But Spanish-Americans lived along this viaduct now; a Spanish lodging house was in nearly every segment. This might be the one, and it might not.

We had seen that there was a young woman in this upper bedroom. The silhouette of her showed again on the drawn blind—a slim, girlish figure with a profusion of hair half falling upon her shoulders.

"Look!" murmured Dirk abruptly. "A man up there—"

We saw now that there was a man in the room with her. It seemed that they were sitting by a table, with the light close behind them.

"That could be Pelegrino," Dirk whispered. "I don't know."

The shadows were monstrously distorted. We could see the blob of a man's head and shoulders, but not much else.

Was it Pelegrino? The man and the woman were evidently in earnest conversation, but the window was closed in spite of the heat of the night, and my electro-audiomagnifier would not reach them. Over our heads one of the great bridges into the Brooklyn district roared with traffic; there was a clanking crane on the level directly beneath us, and the noise was great.

"If you think that's Pelegrino," I whispered, "let's go in and nip him."

"We'll wait—see what happens when he leaves."

"Unless he goes out the rear exit."

"One of us can get in through that side alley."

There was the dark gash of an alleyway between this house and the one next to it. We shifted back behind a catwalk cable-post as a pedestrian went by. Then again the segment was empty. There were few pedestrians along here this Sunday evening. The viaduct was badly lighted—the city here a shambles, a disgrace to its day.

Again Dirk was gripping me.

"That fellow over there—he's after something."

THE MAN down the viaduct had moved; he was standing in plainer view now. And I saw, up at the lighted window, that the shadows of the man and woman were closer together. It seemed that she was leaning toward him, and her arms went up around his neck.

Perhaps it was that which goaded the outside lurking man

into action. We saw him move suddenly forward. He cast furtive glances around, then darted swiftly for the front steps of the house, mounted them, fumbled with the front door, entered and closed it softly after him.

It happened all in an instant. I saw the fellow plainly as he ran across the viaduct. He seemed young—a slight boyish figure. He was bareheaded; as he ran, his gaudy jacket parted, disclosing wide pantaloons, fringed and with a broad tasseled belt tight about his waist. He was a Spanish-American, evidently.

For a moment after he entered the house Dirk and I stood breathlessly watching. We had no desire to make our presence known unless the man in the upper bedroom were Pelegrino. And even against him we had little direct evidence which would hold him for any serious charge. Franklin Dirk was at this time a consulting criminologist in the Federal service; and I—Jac Baker—was his assistant. We had an office here in Great-New York, though our chief supervisor was in Washington.

For two weeks now we had been engaged in the quiet investigation of an affair which, if allowed to go unchecked, would terrorize the port of Great-New York and scandalize America before the shipping interests of the world. The thing, I suppose, had been going on for a year. It began with petty vandalism along the river fronts. There was a time—when my grandfather was my age—that these rivers about Manhattan Island and the Brooklyn and Staten Island water fronts were lined with docks and busy with orderly activities of the port. But the age of the air changed all that. The great trans-oceanic air liners began carrying the passengers, and some of the freight. And the sub-sea freighters were put into service. Surface vessels, buffeted by wind and wave, fell into disrepute.

The rivers, and the upper bay of Great-New York were now a shambles of antiquated docks, literally falling apart. The multiplicity of bridges and viaducts spanning the narrow waters made the neglected little rivers seem almost subterranean as they flowed dark and sullen underneath the spanning network.

I AM no politician. I cannot say why these sections of the city should have received so little care, when all the rest was sleek and shining with a super-modernity. But it was so.

And here, quite naturally, all the disreputable, criminal characters of the population gathered. Perhaps the authorities were pleased to have it that way. Certainly the general public cared not a whit. Crimes of the water front affected the shipping interests; insurance companies were perturbed when, a few months ago, some valuable freight was stolen from a harbor warehouse, almost under the nose of the harbor police. But to the general public—listening to the newscasters—it was merely another example of police inefficiency.

Then the vandalism had grown rapidly worse. The districts were like rabbit warrens of underground and underwater shambles. I think that it surprised the authorities, when once they gave it serious attention, to discover how difficult it could be to maintain order in these mysterious, tumbledown districts. The "Rats of the Harbor," as now they were being popularly called; knew every cubby, every broken dock, every subterranean passage. From petty vandalism, cursed by the underwriters whose purses suffered, the Harbor Rats grew bolder. The small force of the Harbor Police was suddenly demonstrated to be wholly inadequate. There was much talk, but little done about it.

Then, from Washington, Dirk was ordered to investigate conditions. Most especially were we told to make no open display of our activities. Our chief superior—differing from the New York authorities—was of the opinion that the main current of the trouble was not from large numbers of petty, isolated criminals, but rather from a small, highly organized band, armed with money and technical knowledge. Rats they might be, but we felt they were more in the nature of pirates—with a well equipped lair hidden somewhere in the crumbling water front catacombs.

And now, after more than a week, we were upon the trail of one Pelegrino. Dirk had once or twice seen him in the past. We were ordered quietly to nip him, and without noise or publicity—unknown to the water front criminals or even to the Harbor Police—fly him to Washington, for questioning by our superior.

We thought, this Sunday evening, that we had him here in this Spanish lodging house, visiting this woman.

The young Spaniard who, like ourselves, was watching the house, rushed in suddenly. He had no sooner closed the front door when up in the bedroom we saw upon the drawn blind the silhouettes of the two figures in sudden motion. The man was on his feet; the woman was clinging to him. Then he cast her off; his arm came up as though he had struck her.

Dirk took a step or two but stopped abruptly. We had no desire to bring attention upon ourselves by plunging into some meaningless water front brawl.

"Jac! Try the listener again! They're talking louder."

I was fumbling with my apparatus; the man and woman were evidently in a violent altercation. Suddenly a third figure appeared up there. The young man from outside. We saw a knife clutched in his upraised hand. He struck. Then the two men seemed locked together, fighting. The silhouette of the woman vanished from the blind as she fell to the floor. And we heard, muffled from the room up there, her shrill scream.

"Come on," shouted Dirk. "Go 'round the back! I'll take the front!"

I stuffed the little listener-grid into my pocket. We dashed across the viaduct.

Dirk bounded up the front steps, and I plunged into the dark and littered side alleyway.

CHAPTER II

A MYSTERIOUS WOMAN

THE ALLEY WAS very nearly black. The floor of it was strewn with refuse. I stumbled its hundred foot length, along the blank side-wall of the house, and came into an open back yard area. There was more light here—a glow from a few windows of the surrounding houses and from the skyscrapers in the distance. I could see the square, untidy yard, with a six-foot wooden palisade enclosing it. Beside me was a short flight of steps leading to a door, evidently the kitchen of the house.

The place was now springing into turmoil. I dimly heard shouts from the interior. Lights were showing; there was the thud of running footsteps. Dirk and I were armed, this night, only with short-range heat-ray cylinders. Mine was in my hand as I mounted the back steps. From inside I thought I heard Dirk's voicc shouting; and the hiss of his weapon.

I was halfway up the shaky little wooden staircase when above me the door burst outward and a figure catapulted down. It came with such an abrupt reckless leap into the dark that I could not avoid it. I was knocked backward. I found my arms clutching a man. We fell—half falling and half rolling down the steps—ten feet down into the yard.

My cylinder was gone. The breath was knocked out of me. I was underneath and my antagonist jerked and struck at me to free himself. I recall that he seemed slight and frail. I could not see his face—only the outline of his bare head, with flowing dark hair thick about his ears showing against the upper glow of the distant skyscraper lights.

The struggle lasted no more than a moment. My senses were still confused by the fall. I struck with my fist but only caught his shoulder. Then one of his groping hands on the ground must have found a heavy chunk of wood. I heard a panting phrase of triumph in Spanish as he slammed the missile into my face.

It broke my hold upon him, and like a cat he sprang from me and landed on his feet. I was up only in time to see him dashing across the dim yard. With a bound he scrambled over the low palisade and vanished.

I stood, weak and dizzy, with blood streaming down my face from a gash on the cheek. For a moment I heard his swift footsteps as he dashed down the near-by alley, gained a little connecting catwalk to the opposite viaduct and was gone.

From the house Dirk was calling.

"Jac! Are you out there, Jac? Which way did he go? One of them came out here. Are you all right, Jac?"

"Yes—I'm all right."

My head was clearing. Chagrin swept me that I had lost this fellow. He was evidently the young Spanish lad who had been watching the house. The outline of his head and hair was familiar; and in my hand now I found a cloth and tinseled tassel which I had snatched from his belt.

As I turned back toward the steps the figure of Dirk showed in the rectangle of the kitchen doorway.

"He's gone," I called. "Damn me, what an ass. I'm sorry—"

There was a man up there with Dirk, jabbering at him in Spanish; and inside the house a confusion of voices. I found my heat-ray cylinder lying by the bottom of the steps.

Dirk surveyed my bloodstained cheek and rueful smile.

"Good Lord, Jac—he seems to have been a fighter."

"Came out like a rocket and fell on me." I told him what had happened.

Dirk himself had fared no better. He was mounting the interior staircase when the two men had burst from the woman's room. One—my antagonist of the yard—tumbled down a back stairway. The other went up toward the roof, with Dirk after him. The girl in the room was screaming wildly. The other inmates of the house were rushing into the halls. Dirk chanced one reckless shot as he saw his quarry gain the roof. The man evidently knew the lay of the place and Dirk did not. At all events he reached a drainage pipe, dropped to a lower balcony, reentered the house and seemed to have escaped by the front entrance.

"Not so good," grinned Dirk, as he described it. "We'll get no platinum medals for this incident."

He leaned toward me in the kitchen as we stood surrounded by the excited Spanish lodging house keeper, his wife and two or three of the tenants. "Worse, Jac— That was Pelegrino. I'm sure of it now. Come on upstairs—we'll see what the girl in the case has to say."

WE SHOOK ourselves loose and started for the upper bedroom. Dirk told the proprietor to quiet the uproar and not to send for the police.

"No! Me—I want not the police! My house she is respectable." He waved his fat hands and then tore at his hair. "You are the police—you report me, no? Santa Maria—upon my respectable house—"

We got him quiet, and in a moment the uproar was over. From the near-by dwellings people were staring. But a brawl like this was a fairly usual occurrence in this neighborhood—no one had a great curiosity, only a fear that the police would arrive.

"What have you got there, Jac?"

I showed Dirk the tassel. "Ripped it from his belt."

We reached the front second floor bedroom. The girl had stopped screaming. We found an older woman with her now, calming her.

"Leave us," Dirk commanded. "She'll be all right. We want to talk to her."

He displayed his official insigne. The woman mumbled mistrust in Spanish at us, but she left and I slammed the bedroom door after her.

The girl was crouching on the bed. She had been sobbing, but now she lay on one elbow like a trapped animal, gazing at us with sullen, narrowed eyes.

"Do you speak English?" Dirk demanded.

She only stared.

"Do you?" he insisted. His gaze held her. He took a step forward, with his tall lean figure bending over her.

"No, señor," she said at last.

"Because," he added, "if you do not speak English, I shall have to call the Great-New York police."

He said it very slowly and carefully. And, watching her, I could not doubt but that she understood. A new fear came into her eyes.

"But you are the police," she said suddenly.

Dirk relaxed, and flashed me a smile. "Sit down, Jac."

I took a chair. Dirk sat on the edge of the bed beside the girl.

"We are not the police," he retorted. "We are officials from Washington. We were passing the house and heard the noise and came in. I would rather not call the police—if you will answer my questions."

"I know nothing, *señor.*"

"What is your name?"

"Josefa Querida."

She told us that she had been born in Great-New York; that she lived alone here in this lodging house; and that she worked in the plant of a metal industry in South Manhattan. She looked like a factory girl. I saw now that she was very pretty, in a dark, romantically Latin fashion. She seemed hardly more than sixteen or seventeen. Her black hair was tumbling about her shoulders. Her dark eyes and long black lashes were wet now with tears. Her face was pale; the tears had smeared its cosmetics; but her lips, uncolored, were red as a scarlet blossom.

She was wearing a wide pantaloon-skirt, a broad red belt, and a gaudily embroidered blue cotton waist. The waist sleeve was torn, exposing one of her white shoulders.

It was easy to see that we would have a different time with her.

"YOU HAD a man visitor to-night," Dirk said gently. "I see you dressed very prettily for him. How did you tear your dress?"

Her gaze went to it; with one hand she gathered the torn place together, but she did not answer.

"What was the man's name?" Dirk insisted.

"*Señor—*" She stopped. "I—I do not know his name."

"You mean you will not tell me?"

"It was—his name it was Raques Miguel."

"It wasn't Pelegrino, by any chance?"

She was no hardened criminal, this girl. Before Dirk's keen gaze and quiet questions, she was wholly transparent.

"No! Not him—I mean I said he was the name Miguel."

She might just as well have admitted it was Pelegrino. She shrank back on the bed; her frightened gaze swung from Dirk to me. And suddenly I noticed that she was unnaturally holding one of her hands behind her. And I saw that on the red of her belt sash there was a dark stain. I left my chair and stood by Dirk.

"What is she holding her hand behind her for?" I whispered.

He silenced me.

"But, chief, there's blood on her belt—"

"Josefa," he said, "a man named Pelegrino was here with you to-night. You were quarreling—we saw you from the street. Another man—a young man—was out there also. And then he came in. What was that young man's name?"

"No!" she burst out. "I did see no young man! Only Señor Miguel. He quarrel with me. He no love me any more!"

Dirk reached suddenly, gripped her arm, and brought her

hand from behind her. There was blood on it. Her fingers were cut, as though she had gripped a knife-blade.

"*Señor!* Let me go! That—that is nothing. I cut myself!"

Dirk's gentleness momentarily left him. As he rolled the girl over we found the knife upon which she was lying to hide it. I recalled what I had seen on the drawn blind of this room. The young Spaniard who had arrived last had struck at the other man with a knife. In a jealous rage, no doubt, he had tried to stab him. The girl, in the mêlée, had seized the knife-blade.

But we could get nothing out of her. Dirk had been gentle. Now he tried roughness. But she only went into a fit of hysterical weeping.

"*Pero* no—I will no talk!"

"Then I'll send for the police," Dirk declared.

But she sobbed, with her head buried in the pillow, and the threat went for nothing.

"I'd better search the room," I suggested. "See what else might be here."

Dirk nodded. And he sat by the girl, trying to calm her. I pried into her belongings. There seemed nothing of interest. Then on the floor, under the table, with the girl's eyes upon me as I stooped, I found a torn fragment of letter paper.

"Only this, chief."

It was blank on both sides, rumpled, and torn diagonally across. The girl uttered a half suppressed cry as I picked it up.

Dirk held it against the light. It was devoid of writing. Then he smelled it. I knew what that meant—a chemical odor which might suggest invisible ink.

"You think so, chief?"

"Perhaps. We'll see later." He put it in his pocket. "What was that paper, Josefa?"

"*Señor,* nothing. I do not know."

"Never saw it before, eh?"

"No, *señor.*" She was calmer again; watching us with that narrow gauging look.

I folded the knife and placed it in my jacket with the tassel which I had plucked from the young Spaniard's belt. And presently we were ready to leave.

"I won't ask you any more questions," Dirk told the girl. "You only lie to me, so what's the use?"

He smiled, and suddenly she smiled back at him. She was sitting up on the bed now. He touched her cut hand. "Be careful of that, Josefa. Put some antiseptic on it."

"Sí, señor." She added abruptly, "I like you—even you, the police." She hesitated. And then she said impulsively,

"That young man—he was here. He do no harm—I swear it. You—if you sometime meet him—you do not hurt him, no?"

"You love him?" said Dirk. "That's it? Not the other, but him?"

"I—" She seemed to repent her impulsive confidence. "I—*señor,* I never harm you—not anybody. Let me alone."

WE LEFT her presently. As we closed her door, I stood for a moment with my ear against it, listening. I heard her softly sobbing again; and then suddenly she sprang from the bed and was moving about the room. I heard a cabinet drawer open.

"Chief, she's up to something. Why didn't you go after her harder? She knows plenty. You could have dragged it out of her."

"And warned her so that she wouldn't make a move," he whispered. "What was the use of that? She's no fool, that girl. Whatever happened there to-night she may have something now she wants to do about it. Pathetic little thing, too—so young, mixed up in an affair like this. Well, we'll see."

Down the hall there was a vacant bedroom. Dirk drew me into it.

At the staircase head the lodging house proprietor stood anxiously watching us.

"Just a moment," Dirk called to him. "Everything is all right. We're going shortly."

He closed the bedroom door upon us. "See if you can get the office."

I connected my little portable audiphone. We had connection in a minute or two.

"Greenleaf?" said Dirk. "I'm at 89 Rivington, Terrace 3."

Greenleaf was one of our under-officemen. Dirk began talking in our private office code. He described the house, and Josefa told Greenleaf to come at once, properly equipped for shadowing and eavesdropping; and that he was to watch the house, follow Josefa if she came out—and communicate with us at the office at his first opportunity.

"We're going back to the office, then?" I asked as Dirk disconnected.

"Yes. We'll see if that slip of paper has any writing on it. Greenleaf will be here in ten or fifteen minutes—not much chance of the girl getting out before then."

We left the house openly, with sufficient ostentation so that the girl could not fail to know we had gone. Down the viaduct, Dirk changed his mind. We waited long enough for Greenleaf to arrive. He was wearing a magnetic non-reflecting invisible cloak. We could not see him; but he saw us and gave us a faint signal-flash of greeting.

"Good enough," said Dirk. "There he is—over there on that catwalk. Come on, let's get back."

We walked to the nearest moving sidewalk. It was no more than a mile or so to our office in the mid-Manhattan district. As we left the sidewalk for our ascending escalator to our office level, I saw a figure behind us dart back furtively into the shadow of a viaduct sign-grid.

"Chief! Some one is after us!"

We went calmly up the ascent. At the top, instead of proceeding normally, we ran into an arcade doorway—a shop entrance which was dark this Sunday evening.

In a moment the escalator brought up our purser.

It was the young Spaniard who had worsted me in our back yard encounter!

CHAPTER III

THE ASSIGNATION

"**SHALL I NIP** him, chief?" I asked Dirk.

"No."

There were a few pedestrians passing at the time. The fellow had evidently not seen us. He stood, furtively shrinking against an angle of the escalator head, seemingly in doubt as to what to do.

"Come on," murmured Dirk. "Let him follow, if he likes."

We sauntered into the passing pedestrian stream. In a moment we were in our office. From the window I could see the pedestrian viaduct. The young Spaniard was out there, watching our office window-ovals and the arcade entrance.

Dirk had gone at once to his laboratory and I joined him. He was working over the torn fragment of paper.

"That fellow is outside, chief."

"Good. Let him alone."

"Anything on it?"

"I don't know yet."

It proved to be a fairly baffling variety of sympathetic ink, but Dirk finally found that sulphuric fumes with moderate heat brought it out. The writing showed as a dull yellow scrawl. It was only the fragment of a sentence—short lines with the diagonal tear cutting them off.

Pele
See me at

Lat. 41°—'—"
Long. 74°—"
Come subterranean
Sunday night at
Effinstein

The ink faded and was gone as we drew the paper from the fumes of the acid; but it had lasted long enough for me to copy down the words.

We studied them. The message did not seem unduly cryptic. Evidently one Effinstein—of whom we had never heard—had commanded Pelegrino to meet him at a place designated by this latitude and longitude. I have named here only the degrees. The message, however, gave the exact minutes and seconds, of both latitude and longitude.

The time was Sunday night. But at what hour? The note had evidently named the hour, but this fragment did not tell it. This was Sunday night. It could be now. Dirk tried to guess what might have happened in that lodging house room. Pelegrino, we surmised, had come to see the girl Josefa. They had quarreled. Perhaps he did not love her any more, as she said. Or perhaps he was trying to persuade her of something.

"I think," said Dirk, "he showed her this paper—telling her what it meant. Whatever the argument, about that time the fellow from outside burst in on them."

"A jealous lover," I suggested. "He had the knife. He tried to stab Pelegrino, but the girl caught the knife-blade in her hand. Then the uproar frightened both men, so that they stopped fighting and tried to escape."

"Did escape," said Dirk, with his quiet smile. "Having only us two to stop them, they escaped very neatly."

"I wonder what became of the other half of this note."

"I imagine Pelegrino was showing it to the girl—before the young fellow arrived. Let's say she snatched at it, tore it. The other half probably was hidden in her dress—and this piece fell to the floor and she had no time to recover it."

Doubtless the facts were something like that. What it all could mean, we had no idea; but that we had stumbled upon some activity of Pelegrino's was obvious. Our best course seemed to quietly investigate—to follow the clew we had. If only we could have guessed its importance, and the swiftness with which events were destined to develop!

"This Spanish lad," I said, "seems determined to stick to us. What do you make of that?"

Dirk shook his head. "No use theorizing. Put on a cloak and go out and bring him in—if you can find him."

I DONNED one of our magnetic hooded police cloaks. The dark metallic-woven fabric covered me from head to foot. With the current coursing through it, all the light-rays were absorbed. And the light-rays from objects behind it were bent by the aura of its magnetic field, so that the background was undistorted. It gave, for all practical purposes, an invisibility.

Following the side-wall, I passed our main arcade entrance and was upon the viaduct. It was difficult to avoid bumping into the passing pedestrians. But I managed it, keeping close to the parapet. I went a hundred feet or so, and then, ducking to avoid collisions, I gained the escalator head.

The young Spaniard had gone. Or if not, he was well enough secluded so that I could not find him. Invisible cloaks upon occasion are of marvelous help. But on a lighted level, in a crowd, they are more of a hindrance. The parapet lights blurred through my visor. Pedestrians, to whom I was invisible, charged breathlessly at me. I bumped full-head into one old man, left him dazed and bewildered at having found nothingness so solid; and then I gave it up and went back to the office.

"Gone," I said. "We should have nipped him when we had a chance."

Dirk was answering our audiphone buzzer.

"Greenleaf? Yes, this is Dirk. Where are you?"

The muffler was off. I heard Greenleaf's answering microphonic voice.

"East Rivingston—at the Bridge Central approach. Chief, by the gods of the airways, I'm sorry—"

He had lost the girl. A few minutes after we had left the vicinity of the house, she had come out. Greenleaf followed her as she went on foot toward the river front. In a restaurant dive of the "Palace Dance" variety she had met a man.

"Who?" Dirk demanded.

"Chief, I don't know. I never saw him before."

"Describe him. Did you get a decent look?"

Greenleaf had peered at them from a fairly close viewpoint. From his description it sounded like Pelegrino. They had only stayed a few minutes in the restaurant. And when they left, with a sudden alertness come upon them which took Greenleaf by surprise, they got out to the bridge approach where always there is a jam of vehicles and pedestrians—and Greenleaf had lost them.

Dirk cursed his chagrined assistant. "Did they cross to Brooklyn, Greenleaf?"

"I don't think so."

"Did they take a vehicle?"

"Chief, I am honest that I don't know. But I think not."

"Maybe," suggested Dirk sarcastically, "they doubled back on foot and went down to the river front."

"Chief, that might be what they did."

"In fact," added Dirk, "you haven't got the glow of an idea what they did. That's all, Greenleaf. Come back here to the office. We'll be gone, but you wait here. I may send a message in later."

He disconnected. "We're cursed, Jac. Everything we touch goes wrong to-night." He was on his feet. "Get our things ready." He named several articles of our equipment. "Hurry! It's after ten already. That note says Sunday evening. Now, perhaps. He's taken Josefa to the meeting with Effinstein. Wouldn't you say so?"

It was the obvious trail for us to follow. While I got us ready,

Dirk pored over a harbor map. The designated latitude and longitude was on the Island of Staten not far beyond the bottleneck of "Narrows" which connects the Upper Harbor with the main Lower Bay. I glanced over Dirk's shoulder at the map. The old Fort Wadsworth stood within a few miles of this spot.

It was about ten thirty when we left the office. After many days of fruitless prying into Pelegrino's activities, we seemed at last to have come upon a trail. It might lead to something important, and it might not. Yet I recall that just at that moment, as we started for this place down the distant outlying water front where for some unknown purpose Pelegrino was to meet the unknown Effinstein, like a premonition it came to me that we were upon the brink of something big.

If only one might see, even a little hour, into his shrouded future! If that glimpse had been given us, Dirk and I would not have so brashly started alone upon this quest!

CHAPTER IV

STOWAWAY

THE FOOT-CROWD OUTSIDE our office was thinning. I gazed around, but I did not see the young Spaniard and Dirk was in no mood to loiter. For the past two weeks, since our investigation of the activities of the Harbor Rats began, Dirk had had a small high-speed surface boat, equipped for harbor police work, moored on the Hudson water front. It was up near the Seventy-Second Cross-Street.

We started for it now. Dirk called a public fare-car.

"Not too fast," he told the driver.

"We're in no hurry."

"Why not?" I demanded, but he shook his head at me.

"You don't want to take the air?" said the chauffeur. "I can land on the stage at Circle 70 and roll you across from there."

"No," said Dirk. "Roll us all the way. Take the main North viaduct, and cross at Seventy-Second."

"As you say, boss."

We rolled slowly northward into the main traffic stream. Dirk seemed absorbed in his thoughts and I did not bother him. From this upper level I could see the sky now. It was heavily overcast. There was a strong wind from the north.

And a little late? I saw a lightning flare up there as though a summer storm were coming.

We turned west at the Seventy-Second Junction. And as we approached the river we descended to the ground level.

"This will do," said Dirk abruptly. "Let us out here."

The cañon street, lined here with dark shops, was open to the sky. The storm was gathering overhead; a few drops of rain splattered down.

Dirk dismissed our car. There was quite a little traffic here, pedestrians and vehicles heading for the Seventy-Second Cross-Bridge over to Jersey. We proceeded on foot to the river front, with the traffic mounting to the bridge approach so that here on the ground it thinned rapidly. The houses and shops were progressively less pretentious as we advanced. Then we came to a segment of storage buildings, with low-class tenement dwellings intermingled. A large Negro population was here, spreading southward to the Fifty-Third Cross-Street. But it was not a shambles like the water fronts to the south and the east.

We found our little boat undisturbed. Dirk unbolted the dock house door. We lighted no lights, using only our handflashes. It was raining outside now; the rain pounded on the low tin roof.

I loaded in our equipment. The boat sat low in the water. It was some forty feet in length, streamlined and narrow. The engine pit was forward, almost under the flaring razor bow, with a glassite windshield. Behind it, once a bulkhead, was a small storage pit; and behind that, narrowed by the pointed stem, was a pit with half a dozen chairs for passengers. The whole was covered by a low, streamlined cabin roof, with oval glassite windows like ports along its length.

"Ready, Jac?"

"Yes."

I stowed our equipment in the central pit, with the underwater suits and subsea lights which Dirk had already provided. This was a surface boat only, but Dirk had foreseen that at any time we might need submarine apparatus. The interior of the boat was black, save for the reflected silver glow on the instrument panel and the steering wheel. I started the motor. This was a stern side-drive engine, muffled with every latest device. It hummed, almost vibrationless, as the side propellers, with blades uninclined, slid through the water.

I WAS casting our moorings, as we lay purring in the slip. Through the forward windshield I could see the oblong opening of the boat house; the dark river out there, tinted yellow from the glow of the overhead bridge lights.

A distant flash of lightning briefly glared; and after an interval, there came the thunderclap.

"We're going to get it," I said. "Are you carrying headlights?"

"I think we'd better… Wait a minute, Jac." Dirk suddenly climbed through the side-port door to the dock. "Come out here," he added softly.

I switched off the engine. "What is it?" I whispered.

"We'll go over to the entrance—see if any one is in the street outside."

"That Spanish fellow?"

"Maybe."

Without lights we prowled to the boat house entrance, but at once Dirk wanted to return.

"No one here. Let's start. You drive, Jac, and don't saunter."

"Right." I inclined the propeller blades and we slid forward, out of the boat house with a sweeping southward turn into the river. In a moment we were nearly at full speed. The bridge arches overhead went by in a blur. We followed the Manhattan bank. The broken, dilapidated docks lay dark and deserted. Occasionally a local aircraft stage reared itself to the level of the bridge spans. At the Forty-Second Cross-Street, the Jersey monorail spanned the river. We swept under its low-hung span, through the southbound arcade with a rush of wind, and out again into the open in a few seconds.

Dirk had no need to tell me not to saunter. There was a thrill in driving this little ship. She could do a fair eighty miles an hour on the straightaway, with upflung bow and the stern sucked down, her rush so smooth and light that she seemed momentarily on the verge of taking to the air.

There was little river traffic this night; always very little, in fact. We passed a local police patrol, which was heading northward, slanting lazily across to the Hoboken district. They answered our signal, and incuriously let us pass.

It was a drive of only a few minutes to the lower end of Manhattan. To our left the gigantic city reared itself against the leaden sky. The glow from its upper towers mingled with the bridge and viaduct lights and painted the river with a sheen like gold. Monstrous city! Yet it was a wonderful monster—greatest monument in the world to the genius of inventive man. The voice of it carried down here to the river level—the giant murmuring voice of the city, compounded of all the myriad individual sounds, blended now into its throaty voice.

"You're right, we're going to get that storm," Dirk said abruptly. "Head for Bedloe's Island. You can see the Liberty light."

The storm from the north was almost upon us. The lightning and thunder were momentarily more frequent. It was raining harder now, and the wind from up the river brought following waves, boiling with white tops as we cut through them.

The giant, yellow-lighted pile of masonry and metal that marked Lower Manhattan lay behind us. The fairly open Upper Bay lay ahead. A few old-fashioned surface freighters were at anchor along here. Beyond our bow the Liberty Statue light showed with the stage-lights of Staten Island behind it. At shortly after eleven o'clock, from the Brooklyn main air-stage the Chicago night-mail came up and sailed over us, dotted with its red and green speedlights. It ascended with a great upward sweep, through the lower traffic lines which were thin to-night and showed only as little mooring dots of light against the sky; and reaching the 20,000 foot through-traffic level, it soared westward and away.

Dirk seldom spoke as we rushed forward. We would soon reach the latitude and longitude on the Staten shore which the note had given. He suddenly gripped my shoulder. "Sit quiet!"

He left me. Like a cat he climbed back over the little bulkhead steps into the storage pit. What was this? I gazed back, but in the darkness of the boat's interior under the vaulted roof I could not see him.

And then, above the hum of the motor and the wash of the waves against our sides, I heard his voice:

"So there you are! Come out of that!"

There was a scuffle.

"Señor—"

"Come out of that! I've got you, you little idiot—stop struggling!"

Dirk reappeared, floundering forward again, dragging another figure with him.

It was the young Spaniard!

CHAPTER V

UNDER THE WATER!

"NOW THEN," SAID Dirk, "you've damn sure wanted to be with us—and you're here. Are you going to talk, or do I have to pound it out of you?"

"*Señor,* I will talk. Do not hurt me!"

Dirk was holding his heat-cylinder leveled. "I won't hurt you. Give me your weapons."

"I do not have weapons."

But Dirk searched him. "Slow up, Jac," he told me. "We'll see what this fellow has to say."

We were passing the Liberty light. I dropped us to some twenty miles an hour, and sat watching Dirk as he went through our captive's pockets. He was unarmed. We saw now that he was hardly twenty—a handsome little fellow, with a pale face, flashing dark eyes, and wavy, coal-black hair long about his ears.

"What is your name?" Dirk demanded.

"Ramon."

"Ramon what?"

"Ramon—it is not important. *Señor,* you do not know me."

"No," said Dirk, "but we've seen quite a bit of you to-night. Why have you been following us?"

Our captive's gaze was on me. He still looked frightened, but less so than before.

"You're a good fighter," I said abruptly, "for such a little fellow."

"It was you—there in that yard? I am sorry—I was excited."

"Why have you been following us?" Dirk reiterated.

"I want—I want very much—to go where you go."

"Well, you're here. Now what?"

I realized now why Dirk had insisted that our public car go so slowly from the office to the dock; and why he had left the boat alone for a moment just as we departed—giving this Ramon ample opportunity to come with us.

"Now what?" Dirk repeated.

"You—you are the secret police? You are going after a man?"

"Pelegrino," said Dirk abruptly. "Is that who you're interested in?"

The glow from the instrument panel showed Ramon's eyes with a darkling, smoldering light in them. The light of hatred. No one could doubt it.

"Him—yes! You know where he is? Oh, *señor! Señor,* you jus' take me to him!" He was suddenly clutching at Dirk, pleading—"You jus' take me to him!"

"So that's why you've been following us? Because we're after Pelegrino?"

"Señor, sí! You follow him? This piece of paper—he have writing on it, but I do not know how to get it out."

His slim, trembling fingers fumbled in his jacket and he produced the other half of the torn note.

"Señor, I get this! But Josefa she—she tear it, and the rest drop to the floor."

"We found it," said Dirk.

"It had writing?"

"Yes."

"Then you know what Pelegrino do?"

"Some of it." Dirk was holding the other half of the note. "If we only had the chemicals here, Jac! This probably has the hour of meeting on it."

"You go after him now?" Ramon asked.

"Yes."

IT SEEMED to content him. He relaxed, but the smoldering fire remained in his eyes.

"You're good at asking questions," Dirk said. "Suppose you answer a few. What is Pelegrino engaged in to-night?"

"But that I do not know!"

"He is to meet a man named Effinstein," Dirk went on. "Down here along the far-Staten water front. Who is Effinstein?"

"Of him, never did I hear."

His vehemence left no doubt that he was telling the truth. He added suddenly, "I have tol' you all I know. Only that it is something big—something mos' important to-night—that I know. Josefa, she say—"

He suddenly stopped, as though his mention of the girl frightened him.

I said abruptly, "What is Josefa to you?"

"*Señor*, everything! She—she go away with Pelegrino to-night, I think." His clenched fingers on the arm of his seat were bloodless with his grip. "He was telling her she mus' go, very far away with him when this night's work is over. So I know it is important—he try for something big—and with much money then he take Josefa and never will I see her again. *Señor*, he treat her bad—I have try telling her, but she will not listen."

Again he clutched Dirk. "*Señor*, believe me, I am not mix with Pelegrino. Never did I meet him until tonight."

"And then you tried to kill him," I said.

He ignored it, with a dark flash from his eyes. "And, *señores*, you do not blame Josefa? She do nothing. She only think she love him."

"We do not blame her," said Dirk gently. "She is with him now; you didn't know that?"

"With him—now? Oh—" The breath went out of him. He stared at us with anguish in his gaze. "With him—now?

Down here—" He gestured ahead of us, to the approaching Narrows where the dark sullen channel went under the maze of yellow-lighted bridge viaducts connecting Staten with the lower-Brooklyn districts.

"We think so," said Dirk.

I know Dirk had felt a compassion for the wayward Josefa. And to me, there was an equal pathos about this lad Ramon. He seemed imbued with only one idea—to get us to lead him to Pelegrino.

"You will take me, *señores?* You jus' let me get to him! That is all I want—jus' to see him!" His gaze strayed to Dirk's cylinder.

"Here's something of yours," I said. I produced the knife which the girl had been hiding; and as Dirk nodded, I handed it to him.

"Oh, *señor*—"

"It's yours, isn't it?"

"Mine, yes! *Muchas gracias, señores.*"

I had the boat at full speed now. It was still raining. The wind from behind us had increased, kicking up white-capped waves which boiled along our sides. At times the bow would swing high as we overtook and rode a crest, but for the most part I was able to hold us fairly steady. The lightning and the thunder were now almost continuous.

Ramon sat between Dirk and me, staring out through the bow vizor at the rain and the blur of bridge lights. The knife was clenched in his hand.

"I say," said Dirk suddenly, "if you're going into this with us, you take orders from me. Understand?"

"Sí, señor."

"Don't do anything wild. Have you ever been under the water? In a subsea suit?"

"No." It seemed to strike him with terror, but he mastered it. "No, *señor,* never. But I do what you tell me. I am not with fear—only the fear that Pelegrino get away from us."

"You take your orders from me, remember that."

"But yes, *señor.* Jus' what you tell me, I do."

I doubted it.

"Good!" said Dirk. "Keep quiet now. We'll be there presently."

WE SWEPT under the arching bridges. To left and right the great tiers of the Brooklyn and Staten districts rose against the black sky—a blurred yellow glow through the rain and murk. Then the lightning flares would brighten everything for a moment, to disclose the great South Brooklyn aircraft stages where the transatlantic air liners came down.

I had thought the lightning fairly distant, when suddenly there was a flare and a crash. A white glare, blinding—and a sizzling, tingling crack. I thought we had been struck. It was a surprise to find myself still conscious, with Dirk and Ramon still beside me, and the blackness again upon us.

"Lord!" exclaimed Dirk. "That hit our stern!"

It seemed so. The engine faltered momentarily, then was running again. Dirk clambered back the length of the plunging boat, and in a moment returned.

"No damage, but I guess it struck us. We don't want any more like that."

We were hugging the Staten side of the channel. Disreputable shambles of water front here! We passed the grassy towering ramparts of the old Fort Wadsworth; and beyond it the tumble-down catacombs of broken wharfs and docks began again.

We swept from under the channel bridges and came again into the open, with the dark and storm-lashed waters of the Lower Bay before us. Farther out, over our port bow, opposite the Atlantic Highlands and the Hook, by the Coney Island where once was what they called an "amusement park," the main Great-New York air-stage reared itself high above the surrounding buildings. But it was hardly visible now; its beacon lights were almost gone behind the murk. The broad expanse of the Lower Bay showed only a few channel lights, with the huge white beacon of the Hook like a single round eye dominating them all.

"Slow a little," said Dirk suddenly. He was studying his chart, and trying to angle our position with an electro-compass finder. Exactitude was impossible this night. The finder could not give seconds of latitude and longitude. And this dark Staten shore—with its old warehouses, piers and little wooden buildings which marked the various water front activities of a bygone age—had no distinguishing markers by which we could identify our exact position on the chart.

"It's along here somewhere," said Dirk. "On the water front, or it could be in the open bay."

The note had used the words: "come subterranean." It seemed to imply a choice of entrances, so we felt that Effinstein's hidden lair must be on the shore, with both a land and an underwater entrance.

"Angle us with the Hook light," I suggested.

"And what else?" demanded Dirk.

There was indeed no other known point visible to us now. Exact orientation was impossible.

"Ease us over," Dirk added.

"We'll find a place to land here."

FOR A few minutes past we had been running without lights. At low speed I turned us toward the shore. Immediately in the trough of the running waves, we began tumbling and rolling. One white crest lashed up with a surge of white almost over the cabin roof. Ramon gave a low exclamation of fright.

"Don't blame you," muttered Dirk. "Easy, Jac, don't wallow us."

I slanted to take the waves diagonally upon our stern quarter. Dirk and I sat tense, peering through the visor where the arc of the swinging cleaner kept a small segment clear of the pelting raindrops. The shore was only a hundred feet or so ahead of us now. It was a blur of dark, dilapidated structures. A glow of yellow lighted windows showed abreast of us—some public house festively lighted.

"Farther along," Dirk murmured. "Don't head in there."

We did not dare use our search beam. A surface vessel coming in here on a night like this would cause too much comment. We could only hope that the lightning—which for the moment was less frequent—would not disclose us.

I hope that never again do I have to make such a landing. We passed, by a good quarter of a mile, the lighted house. I began praying for a lightning flash to show me something of what lay ahead, but none came.

"In, Jac!"

There was the black blur of a dock, with a dangling roof almost over us, a vague line of white where the waves were pounding. I missed the end of the dock by inches as we reared up on the crest of a wave; and I swung sharp for the shore. We rounded that dark pile of timber, Heaven knows how, slid under a broken catwalk which hung between this dock and the next, and came to a standstill in a dark patch of quiet water under the lee of the frowning wharf.

"Fair enough!" said Dirk. "We can tie up over there to the right. Slide us in."

I was shaking from the strain of it. Ramon sat grim and pale, but Dirk was only triumphant. We found where once had been a small boathouse, inshore beside the larger wharf. It was sheltered from the rough water. I slid us half in, just as a brilliant lightning flash came with almost simultaneous thunderclap. But we were fairly well hidden here.

Were we near Effinstein's place? We could not tell. Nor had I any idea how the spot might be recognized even if we did reach it.

But Dirk had more information than I. "There was an Effinstein listed in the audiophone directory some ten years ago. A stone and cement company—with a place somewhere near here. I'll get our suits ready. Take a look around the shore, Jac."

Ramon said quickly, "And I will go?"

"You stay here," Dirk commanded.

I left them and prowled the shore. By day, there was some business activity along here. Back a hundred feet or so from the line of docks was a dirty, old-fashioned street. I saw not a single pedestrian, and only a very occasional window lighted. The storm had now settled into a heavy downpour of rain and lashing wind, but there was no more lightning. I followed the street for a distance. Then I went again to the wharfs, heading back toward Dirk. The shore front was wholly black. Very cautiously I used a little search beam.

I was about to give it up and go back to our boat. I was only a few hundred feet from it when my light-circle landed upon a sign:

EFFINSTEIN CONSTRUCTION CO.

So this was it! The building was a three-story stone affair, square and solid. It stood on the water front, with the waves pounding its front wall. A dock or a pier had once been there, but it was gone now. The building, though in fair repair, had an aspect of long disuse. The sign was old-fashioned and weather-beaten. The heavy windows were all closed and solidly barred.

Behind the building there was a yard, inclosed by a broken wooden palisade. Rusted machinery stood about, long neglected—what might have been a stone crusher, with a large hopper above, and a screen slide down one side. Near it was an ancient mechanical shovel.

I PROWLED cautiously around. If any one was here, I saw no evidence of it. At the back end of the yard was a little metal house of newer design. It suggested a small office. Its door bore a label, unlighted now:

ISAAC EFFINSTEIN

Perhaps here, by day, this Effinstein conducted some humble but legal little business. A blind for his real activity, I could not doubt.

I was back at our boat in ten minutes more, and told Dirk what I had found. He had three of the diving suits already assembled.

"It's under water, Jac. That's all a blind, as you say. There could be an elaborate subterranean place there—it would stand little chance of discovery."

I could well understand that. Most of the subsea freighters docked farther out now. A few years ago, however, many of the smaller ones put in along here. Submarine structures were common. This whole place, under water as well as above, was a catacomb. And police officials, stumbling upon the illicit equipment of prosperous criminals, are not always above bribery.

It was nearing midnight now. We were into the suits in a moment. Ramon's face was white and grim as I buckled on his round, goggled helmet.

"Do what I've told you," I whispered. "You'll be all right—it isn't difficult to operate. Almost fool-proof—and in a few minutes you'll forget the strangeness."

He tried to smile, and then, through the visor by the glow of his interior headlight, I saw him set his jaw.

Dirk's gloved hand, with its metal finger tips, touched the metal plate on my shoulder and gave us audible contact.

"Ready, Jac?"

"Yes."

Our double-shelled suits, with the pressure nullifying current surging in the wire mesh lining, were bloated with our interior air. I saw, through my glassite panel, the grotesque figures of Dirk and Ramon—shapelessly bloated, with the air-renewers and batteries a great lump on their shoulders, and the goggled helmets making them look like strange monsters of the deep. Dirk's instruments hung, like my own, dangling from his broad belt. Ramon had none—we found he did not know how to use them. But in his gloved hand he clutched his knife.

With Dirk leading us, we let ourselves over the side of the boat and sank into the dark waters of the bay.

CHAPTER VI

IN THE DEPTHS

A SOLID BLACKNESS confronted me. We sank down, weighted by our shoes and belts, and in a few moments I felt the oozy bottom underfoot. It was deeper than I had expected; the tiny dial on the inside of my helmet registered forty-two feet.

Dirk's small hand-flash thrust a twenty-foot blurred beam through the water and showed a moldering, barnacled line of piles supporting the little boathouse; and behind them the larger piers of the dock structure.

Ramon was standing, bracing himself as though he were in a wind and about to blow away. I saw Dirk sway toward him, touch him and speak. Then Dirk came to me.

"We must be careful to keep together. Just my one light—I'll lead—you and Ramon follow."

He swayed in advance of us with plodding steps, his beam swinging in a slow arc.

The bottom to our left went down a steep undulating slope into the deep waters of the bay. To the right, as Dirk's beam struck that way, the slope ascended into shallow water. I saw the stone foundations of a shore front building.

We plodded for ten minutes or more, fairly parallel to the shore. But we were gradually descending. Occasional fishes, surprised by our light, stared and darted away, or flipped past our visors in a panic of fright. Underfoot, crabs scurried for their holes in the ooze.

Dirk was cautious. He sent his beam only occasionally

shoreward; and twice, for minutes at a time, he extinguished it completely, so that we swayed forward blindly against a yielding wall of blackness.

Eerie walk indeed! So black and soundless, yet overhead, no more than sixty feet now, the surface was lashed with wave and wind, and pelted with rain…

I found Ramon touching me.

"A light! You see it?"

Away to the left, far down the descending slope, a faint red light showed—a dull, blurred blob of color. It vanished; but then, as I stared, it came again, glowed and again was gone. I recognized it then—one of the main submarine channel markers for the smaller submarines which sometimes ascended to moorings near the Brooklyn side of the Narrows. It swung with a ten-second flash.

"It's all right, Ramon. Keep going."

Again Dirk's beam came on. He was waiting a few steps ahead of us. He touched me.

"How much farther would you say, Jac?"

"A little—not much. I can't tell."

It was so different down here, from up on the land! But I felt that we must be perhaps a hundred feet or so out from the shoreline and very nearly abreast of the Effinstein building.

Dirk started again. He had shortened his beam's range. I think that it barely carried ten feet. I found us abruptly swaying down a steep incline. The surface was now seventy feet over us. Then eighty. Then in the nineties… We almost stumbled upon the wreckage of a submerged catwalk, which lay on the bottom in a tangle of broken, twisted girders and cables. We clambered over it, like beings upon a strange planet with so little gravity that a leap sent us swinging upward with flailing arms and legs.

I touched Dirk. "There's something shoreward. Do we dare shine on it?"

The blurs, as our light cautiously illumined them, showed a tangle of girders, cables and metal bulkheads. It had once been

The battle was no less deadly because it was silent.

some sort of a submarine mooring place, but it seemed abandoned now. We passed it, heading outward, down the slope. The shoreline now showed other submerged structures. Dirk's care with his light gave us only a vague glimpse. But there was a catacomb here. And suddenly I realized that we were fronting not submarine wreckage, but underwater structures perhaps now in use.

"Chief—"

Dirk came to the same swift realization. Our light vanished; solid blackness and silence again enveloped us.

Dirk's voice said into my ear:

"This must be the place. Stand quiet. Perhaps we'll see a light, or I can raise some sound. I'll try the amplifiers."

I felt him kneeling at my feet, and Ramon was gripping me.

"Señor—"

"It's all right, Ramon. This seems to be the place. We're trying to find out if any one is around here."

I CROUCHED down with Dirk. It is difficult to operate underwater amplifiers, but presently he had them working. I made contact with him. The sounds came up first—a multiplicity of magnified murmurs and muffled rumbles and thuds. The voice of the bay. We could hear the blur of the pounding waves against the shore; the swish and sucking of the water. A million little sounds, individually indistinguishable, blending into a sodden, sullen throb; and from far distant, the hoarse, intermittent blare of a submarine siren, out near the Hook in the main channel. But there was nothing suggesting human activity.

And we amplified the light-glows. The summer phosphorescence inherent to the water became visible as a silver sheen. The red glow from the channel marker in the distance was apparent. From overhead there was the brief vague reflection of a flash, as though a lightning flare had come up there.

But, down here in advance of us, no evidence of humans. Yet in that I was wrong. Dirk's gloved hand made a gesture.

"Lights ahead of us, Jac! Very dim—and I think not very far."

Once more we were standing in total blackness, and in a moment Dirk began swaying forward again. I found the ooze bottom sloping steeply downward. A hundred feet of depth; and presently it was a hundred and fifty. Still no light sheen showed ahead. And then we saw it! A blurred little glow. It was below us, as though we were standing upon a rise of ground. And as we advanced, the glow narrowed; divided into two blobs of blurred light.

I realized abruptly that I could distinguish the outlines of things before me. And there was light enough to show the dark bloated figures of Dirk and Ramon; Dirk with his underwater electro-gun in his hand, and Ramon clutching his knife. I took my own gun from my belt. It would fling, for a distance of ten feet or so, a tiny electronic bolt capable of shocking into insensibility any antagonist.

"There's the place, Jac."

My eyes, with something to focus upon, gradually disclosed the scene. We were standing upon the brink of a little cauldron—a thirty foot depression with sloping sides. At its bottom lay a metal building, low and rambling as though it might have several rooms. The light-sheen was coming from within, through two of its goggling bull's-eye windows. And I saw two circular doors, like the entrances to pressure ports.

The building had a tunnel arcade, running up the slope, shoreward. I could fancy that the tunnel might lead upward, into the cellar of the deserted stone building on the shore which once housed the Effinstein Construction Company.

Every moment I was seeing more. Beyond the low building, in the bottom of the cauldron where there seemed a dredged gully cut downward toward the deeps of the bay, I could vaguely distinguish the outlines of girders, a metal bulwark, and a huge round pressure-shield facing seaward. A submarine mooring port hidden down here? It seemed so. It appeared to be very large, with space enough for any of the subsea freighters.

I suppose we stood gazing only a moment or two. I heard Dirk's tense voice:

"We'll try and get up to one of those windows. No one seems to be out here—"

We moved slowly down the slope toward the sheen of light from the bull's-eye panes. What would we see within this dark, mysterious, underwater lair? Had Pelegrino already arrived? And was the girl, Josefa, with him? What were they plotting down here? We might be able to eavesdrop, with our amplifier contacted to the metal wall of the building.

"Señores!"

Ramon's outflung hands gripped Dirk and me. I felt a swish of the water against my bloated suit. A light flashed with a blinding glare into my visor.

From the blackness, dark bloated figures swayed and surged upon us!

CHAPTER VII

A DESPERATE WARNING

THE ATTACK HAD come wholly without warning, save for Ramon's sudden outcry. The blurred beam was dazzling. A figure struck against me with a swirl of water. A bolt flashed; I felt the tingle of its aura and there was a rain of tiny sparks within my helmet.

Outside, through the visor-pane, I was aware of a blurred confusion. I lurched from the impulse of the figure that had struck me, lost my balance, and sank prone. Over me, bloated forms were fighting. I could not distinguish Dirk and Ramon from the enemy; I did not dare loose my bolt. But another soundless flash leaped past—from Dirk's weapon perhaps.

I regained my feet. A figure holding a light came at me—a giant form leaning against the water with his swift forward rush. But Ramon intercepted him. I saw Ramon's knife descend; and the giant bloated suit suddenly deflated with an outbreak of bubbles. The light dropped and was extinguished.

The alarm must have reached the submarine structure. The window lights had vanished.

In solid blackness I moved forward. I had thought that, off to the left, Dirk was struggling with two or three of the enemy. They seemed to have been dragging him down the slope.

A moment passed. Soundless, solid blackness enveloped me. Yet a fight was going on here—Ramon and Dirk struggling, while I by some stray chance was now unmolested, out of the conflict and unable to get back into it. I went several feet ahead;

then back. Then, with hand-torch levelled, I pressed the contact, but no light came. My torch was out of order.

It seemed that I could feel the current-swirl of water where figures had passed. Should I take the time to connect my sound-amplifier? That seemed futile. Instead, weapon in hand, I strode forward down the slope. I thought that soon I would come upon the building. I took a dozen groping steps. Two dozen…

There was suddenly, to my right, a glow of light. It was a hundred feet away—at my own level now. I saw it to be a round pressure-port of the building, swinging open and with an interior light shafting out. I was not at all where I thought I was. I had headed, not toward the building, but down the slope toward the outer bay!

It was too late now. The pressure-port opened. Its interior water was flooded with light. I saw two figures, dragging another. They flung him in and went in after him; and the round port panel closed upon them.

Was it Dirk, made a prisoner? I feared so. And where was Ramon?

Again I was in solid blackness. But this time I had my direction. At full speed I started for the building. Then caution came to me. Exterior guards had set upon us—and others might still be near by. I moved warily now.

Suddenly a glow from one of the windows came streaming out again. It was hardly thirty feet distant; its reflection laid a very dim sheen through the turgid waters.

No evidence of Ramon. I advanced slowly, keeping out of the direct lightbeam; and presently I was near the bull's-eye of the window. But I did not dare make contact to look in—any one inside would readily have seen me.

There seemed no outside guards now. I saw a very faint reflected light marking the second bull's-eye, some ten feet from me. I moved toward it, reached it.

I FOUND that I was peering into a dim room. It was lighted only by a reflection from the doorway which stood open and showed me a segment of the room adjoining. People were there—a group of them around a low metal table which held a small shaded tube-light. I saw Dirk! He had been divested of his underwater suit. He sat slumped in a chair. His arms and hands were free, but I saw that his legs were strapped to the chair-posts.

From the side angle at which I was gazing only a narrow crescent of the lighted room was visible. There seemed perhaps half a dozen or more men moving about the place. What they were doing I could not determine. I saw Dirk's watching gaze following them. Occasionally one would pass in front of him. Then two of them came into this darker room at the window of which I was standing. They poked about, lifted something from the floor. It seemed a piece of heavy apparatus. They carried it away, beyond my line of sight.

Most of them were big, burly ruffians, with close clipped hair. They were garbed in dark garments—several with narrow leather trousers and tight-fitting black leather jumpers suggesting cargo-loaders. One or two wore the characteristic black, peaked cap.

And there was a woman here. I recognized none of the men save Dirk, but the woman was the girl, Josefa. I could only see her head and shoulders as she sat against the distant wall of the lighted room, with the table between me and her. Amid all the talk and confusion which was going on, she sat silent, and often with her gaze upon Dirk.

How long I stood there I do not know. There was no sign of Ramon. Had he been captured? Was he imprisoned in here, in one of these other, dark rooms? Or was he killed, lying outside on the harbor bottom, near the guard he had stabbed? I could not tell. The men were all talking; busily engaged in preparing for something. But what? Dirk evidently knew by now. I could see how narrowly he was watching and listening. Something was in progress. There was an aspect of haste and tenseness about the scene.

I did not see Pelegrino. He seemed not here. But there was one wizened little fellow with gray-black hair and a hooked nose whom I thought might be Effinstein.

I suppose I saw all this in a moment or two. I was trying to arrange my sound-amplifier. By contacting with this metal wall I might be able to hear the voices.

Presently one of the men was standing in front of Dirk. They were exchanging words, and the standing man cuffed Dirk in the face. Immediately there was a turmoil. Two other men came. The three of them menaced Dirk. One held a knife.

I stood helplessly out there, with my heart pounding in my throat. It seemed that Dirk was about to be killed. I caught a glimpse of his pale face as he stared grimly up at his captors. But the girl Josefa jumped to her feet, with eyes flashing. Whatever she said, it seemed to carry a command. The wizened little Jew abruptly appeared. He sided with the girl.

The three men assailing Dirk were dispersed.

I had my amplifying tubes almost connected; the little grid was contacted with the slimy metal wall against which I was leaning. Would my glowing tubes disclose me? I had to chance it. But before I was quite ready with the connection I became aware that one of Dirk's hands, dangling at his side by the chair, was making finger signs. I caught the letter J. Another, A. And another, C.

Jac!

He was signaling my name! And then swiftly spelling other words! Doubtless he had been doing it for minutes past, on the chance that I was watching. His hand was down near the floor.

NOW I did not contact with my amplifier; I stood breathlessly watching Dirk's swiftly moving fingers. A message! A command for me! He knew now in what this band of ruffians was engaged—and he was trying to tell me!

"Jac! Warn them! Jac! Jac—"

It seemed the end of the message. He spelled my name half a dozen times. And then he began again.

"Jac! The Nemo arriving main channel now with platinum cargo. Send call for help and go now warn the Nemo. Pirate attack. Warn them. Jac! Jac! J..."

He was beginning again. A pirate attack upon the Nemo! She was the largest of the trans-atlantic subsea freighters. I knew that she was due tonight from Liverpool.

Heaven knows the message from Dirk was clear enough. The Nemo was bringing a platinum cargo—a bank transference from England to the United States, undoubtedly. She was due at the Hook now. Pelegrino and other members of this band of harbor pirates had already left to attack her. Effinstein and these others were waiting here for their return. This, then, was what Pelegrino had hinted to Josefa; wanting her to join him tonight. As Ramon had said, when this night's work was done, and the loot disposed of, Pelegrino would take Josefa far away.

For a moment I watched to be sure that Dirk was adding nothing to his message. He was going through it again, with the wording the same. I turned from the bull's-eye. It was a wrench to leave him; but my being there added nothing to his safety.

I leaned against the water, treading out to avoid the slanting beam from the lighted port. I must get up to our boat at once. I could only guess at the time. Probably after midnight now; and upon most of her passages the Nemo flared her signal for the main channel entrance to the Hook by midnight. And the harbor pirates, with what sort of an undersea or surface craft I could not guess, were out there ready to attack her!

The light from Effinstein's lair faded and was gone in the turgid water behind me. Again I was in that solid, soundless blackness. I tried my handtorch futilely. With an agony of apprehension I feared I would lose my direction; there was only the feel of the oozy slope of the bottom to guide me. I plowed along. It seemed an eternity. Floating seaweed fouled my outstretched arms, but I cleared it away. I did not want to ascend to the surface until close upon our boat. Would I find it there? Or would the pirates have discovered it?

Haste was vital. With Dirk now left behind, all my thoughts rushed to the Nemo. If I could gain our boat, I would run it for the main-channel entrance. It was only a few miles from here. And simultaneously I could send out a call to police headquarters for help. And help for Dirk…

With my belt and shoe-weights at last discarded, I shot to the surface and floundered to a broken wharf. I was not far from our boat. I found it in a few minutes—found with a rush of relief that it had not been disturbed.

The storm was still raging. There was no lightning now, but the wind and rain were heavier than ever. The bay was lashed white by the waves! And over them rolled a murk of rain and flying spume. With my underwater suit discarded, I hastily cast off the boat.

And in a moment I was heading out into the storm-tossed darkness, steering for the distant main channel entrance, with only the blurred round eye of the Hook beacon, dim and bleary, to guide me.

CHAPTER VIII

PIRATES' TREACHERY

I HAD BEEN out here many times before, of course, but never upon such a night as this. Distance was difficult to calculate. The lights of the buildings and the stages on the heights of Staten were in a moment lost behind me. I could not see the South Brooklyn shore, nor the Coney Island field-lights; off my starboard bow there was only the Hook beacon—the smaller lights of the Atlantic Highlands were all lost and gone in the blur of the storm.

Within a minute or two I was in a desolation of open, tumbling water. The wind was on the port stern quarter. I was traveling much faster than the rolling white waves—slanting across them. At times the little boat would reach a crest and hang there, then surmount it and coast like a glider down the slope, with the wave-top boiling and sizzling sternward. I seemed alone out here. What little traffic there might have been was too far away for its lights to show. I was not running dark now, but carrying the legal red and green peak signals.

It would be, I judged, no more than eight or ten miles to the surface entrance of the main ascending channel. The Nemo could have arrived there some time ago. Had she? I strained my gaze through the darkness for her signal flare. Were the pirates out here? Would they have a surface craft, braving this storm; or were they in a bandit submarine, lurking somewhere here in the green-black depths, awaiting their chance to attack the freighter?

As soon as I got away from the Staten shore, I connected the boat's audiphone sender. I should have raised the Manhattan wave-sorter in a moment. But I did not. It seemed, as Dirk had said, that everything we touched this night was cursed. I called and called, but to no avail. With sinking heart I remembered that lightning bolt which had seemed to strike us on the voyage out, making the engine momentarily falter. It had deranged the audiphone sender. I was helpless to communicate with the city!

But perhaps the boat's telegraph code-sender would operate? In a panic of apprehension I connected the transmitter. It was equipped to send, but not to receive—an emergency apparatus for use in distress.

The current went into it. The tubes glowed. Steering with one hand, my attention divided between the stormy darkness ahead and the little transmitter beside me, I sent my call.

"Harbor Police Headquarters! Nemo in main channel attacked by pirates! Send help!"

My tiny aerial hissed and snapped. The message was going into the air. Or was it futilely weak? I could not tell. I sent it twice, alternated with a call for help for Franklin Dirk; and I gave the latitude and longitude of the pirates' subterranean lair.

If only my message could get through! With the audiphone dead, the air was so bafflingly silent! I waited five minutes or so. I was well down the bay now. The waves were rolling higher; the wind seemed stronger than ever. Far distant, to port, a red surface beacon marking the surface of the main channel had become visible. It was a second point of orientation to check with the Hook beacon; and when I applied the angles to the chart, it gave my approximate position. I had calculated fairly correctly. The main channel entrance was only a few miles ahead of me.

Then I sent my distress call again. It seemed so futile! I thrust the thought of Dirk from my mind. If the Nemo had not yet arrived, and I could reach her before the pirates attacked—

I was suddenly aware of lights in the murk behind me! A vessel seemed about a mile astern. I gazed back through the stern visor, and saw red and green peak lights, and a little V-shaped masthead glow. They were rapidly brightening. I was being overhauled.

Was it the oncoming pirate craft? For a moment I thought so; and with all my lights out I swung sharply to port. Perhaps they had not seen me—or would ignore me, and go past. I could not stop them. This little boat of Dirk's had no armament; I was armed only with my short-range flash-gun.

THE LIGHTS of the oncoming vessel rapidly increased in brilliance. I saw, presently, a glow along the gunwales, and then the outline of the craft itself. It would pass within a few hundred yards of me—a long, low, black-hulled boat, with squat wings raising its bow so that only the sucked-down stern touched the water.

And suddenly triumph swept me. This was the Health Officers' aquaplane! The Nemo had not yet arrived, but was expected now; and the Port of Great-New York health officials—with the harbor pilot also—were heading out to meet her at the channel entrance.

I was in time with my warning! I flashed on my lights, swung in an arc to starboard, and sent up a boarding signal-flare. Would they stop? I thought at first that they were going past. Then, when almost abreast of me, from the dark low rail of the rakish aquaplane an answering flare went up. The bow sank as the engines were stopped. And across the choppy, lashing waves I headed for her.

It would have been almost impossible, as both boats wallowed in the trough of these seas, for me to board the health plane. I did not try it. But at fifty feet I hailed them. Half a dozen white-clad figures—in the summer uniform of the health officials—were gathered at the lee rail, sheltered from the rain by the overhanging upper deck.

"I'm Jac Baker, Washington Bureau of Criminology," I called. "Hear me?"

"Yes." One of them produced a small electric megaphone. It flung the answer clearly. "Yes. What do you want?"

I had to keep headway. Wallowing in the trough of these white-capped rollers, it seemed that my little boat would be engulfed. I shouted my warning of pirates about to attack the Nemo. I thought that one of the men at the rail laughed sardonically. Didn't they believe me?

"True!" I shouted. "God's truth. My audiphone's out of order. I've tried to call for help—I don't know if it got through. Call the Harbor Police! Call for help!"

"All right!"

I was swinging toward the aquaplane's bow. I shouted again.

"Is the Nemo out there?"

"Yes. Expected now."

"Then go warn her. The pirates are here somewhere—here under the surface, probably." I rounded the bow, and came down along the other side. The officials had crossed to this other rail.

"We'll throw you a line. Tow you."

"All right," I agreed. "From the stern, could you pull me aboard?"

"No. Too dangerous." And some one said, and the megaphone caught it and flung it to me:

"Stop this cursed nonsense. We've got to get started."

And another voice: "Tow him. Pull him in when we reach the sub. I'll attend to—"

"You call the Harbor Police," I bawled. Officials are so often blindly stupid with anything beyond their own little routine! "My chief, Franklin Dirk, is captured." I gave them the latitude and longitude of Effinstein's lair. Told them again that Dirk was a prisoner there.

I passed astern of the plane and caught their cable. Out in the murk ahead of us a yellow rocket signal went up. The Nemo had arrived! She had risen to the surface, at the entrance to the main channel, and was waiting for the pilot and these health officers to board and clear her.

The engines of the aquaplane started. My tow-cable tightened. In the boiling wake my little boat sat stiffly up like a towed surf-board. Through the darkness beyond the bow of the plane-boat I could see the dying flare of the Nemo's rocket. And then, a few minutes later, the lights of her turret were visible.

WE SWEPT, within five minutes, abreast of her; rounded and prepared to make contact. We were not too late. The Nemo was safely here; the pirates had not yet attacked. I saw the length of the vessel's deck—a great black dolphin lying there, with sleek curving back almost awash.

The captain and his chief officer were standing in the bow at the low rail, by the little tower. The stern was down, with lashing waves rolling unchecked over it, and a line of white spray almost amidships, like reef shoals upon which waves were breaking.

The submarine's landing gear was out and ready in her lee bow. The aquaplane slid up, contacted, and was held by the boarding chains.

I was busy with my own problems when the tow-cable slackened. A man from the stern of the plane shouted:

"Run up 'ere aside us."

The rain and the wind had eased off. I heard him plainly. I was busy casting off the cable, steering and starting my motor. But I saw, through the visor, the health officers boarding the Nemo. Five or six of them swarmed the landing gear. The captain and his underofficer met them, on the deck by the tower.

And suddenly there was a flash. The captain of the Nemo wavered and fell!

What was this? The blood seemed to flow like ice in my veins. And now I knew what it meant. What accursed, fatuous stupidity I had shown!

On the dim deck of the Nemo, with its row of tiny lights along the rail, figures from the aquaplane were swarming. The Nemo's chief officer leaped over the captain's prone body, drew a weapon and fired. There were two other simultaneous flashes. The chief officer and one of his assistants fell. From the tower came a flash. But the boarding figures—there seemed a score of them suddenly appearing from the aquaplane—swarmed onto the Nemo; rushed for its tower; leaped for its opened hatchway where the startled crew were coming up.

It all happened in a moment while I was casting off my towline and starting the boat's motor. My accursed stupidity! The pirates had captured this health department vessel at its moorings on shore, and in this guise had come out to surprise the Nemo. Towing me, while I shouted of pirates and told them to call the Harbor Police!

I had my lone little flash-gun lying on the seat beside me. The impulse of the towing had run me within twenty feet of the aquaplane, with my boat wallowing in its lee. I took a shot through the starboard visor, which chanced to be open. Perhaps I hit the figure, running across the plane's top deck. Then an answering shot came—a tiny dazzling heat-flash. It struck, not me, but the instrument panel. The motor went dead with its ignition coils fused.

Then another flash came. Electronic, this time. I only caught its aura, or I should not be alive now. There was a blinding shower of multi-colored sparks; a soundless chaos, with all my senses reeling... I was vaguely aware of falling over backwards from the steering seat... Then I slid, seemingly into an eternity of empty darkness...

CHAPTER IX

FATE UNKNOWN

"LET 'IM UP. Give 'im air."

"The hell! There ain't no air."

"He iss all right, yes? You go ask Pelegrino what we do with heem."

"Hell! I'd knock 'im on the head an' be done with it."

"The big boss he say no."

I saw three or four of the ruffians bending over, watching me as I regained my senses. I came floating back from the void of emptiness. Voices first, then the dim outlines of the men. By a faint blue tube-light I saw their stooping figures—men in ill-fitting white uniforms which they had stolen from the health department.

"So he got his senses? Get away, you. Get back to your work."

The men scattered. Another man loomed over me—a huge burly fellow with a bullet head of close clipped hair. The light gleamed on his heavy jowled face—the features of a foreigner. He wore a short white linen jacket and white trousers, gold-striped. Both were dirty and torn, wet with rain and matted with blood. His face was blood-streaked; a cut across his forehead was tied with a blood-soaked bandage. To me there came the thought of a pirate of old, swaggering amid the carnage of his quarter-deck. But this was modernity. Instead of a picturesque knife in his teeth, I saw dangling from his grease-soaked belt an array of cylinder weapons.

Was this Pelegrino? From the command in his tone as he dispersed the three men, it seemed so.

"Are you got your wits?"

"Yes," I said.

"Not hurt much?"

"No."

"What were you doing out in that boat?"

I did not answer. He bent lower over me. He was grinning sardonically.

"You now very kindly tell us all your business! So you have a partner back now with Effinstein?"

I thought it better not to answer that one either.

He straightened. "You need not spik. We go now to Effinstein. You an' your partner—*finis.*"

His gesture was so expressive I had no need to guess at his meaning.

He called: "Ruffo?"

"Señor." Another figure appeared from near at hand.

"You stay, guard him." The English was doubtless for my benefit. "Not hurt him. Effinstein and me—we fix him and his partner together."

They both chuckled. Pelegrino—if it was he—wandered away. My guard sat down on the steel-grid floor near me with a weapon across his knee, but he did not offer to speak.

With my returning senses I had at first been engrossed by the voices and the figures. Gradually I realized that I was burned and electronically shocked, but not greatly injured. I was lying on a grid-floor. The half-paralyzed quivering of my muscles gradually left me, and I could feel my strength coming back. My apparatus and single weapon were gone.

I saw now that I was lying in a dimly blue-lit concave room. The interior of the Nemo, obviously. Four small metal bunks were here. A catwalk lay along the ceiling overhead, passing in and out of the room through narrow ceiling openings. Under it, an oval doorway gave me a vista of what seemed the engine room.

The Nemo was moving. This whole interior was throbbing and humming with sounds—the pulsing engines, the hiss and throb and sucking of the pressure pumps. And over it I could hear the clanking tread of the men and their calling voices. There were two or three in the engine room within sound of me. Others at intervals scurried along the ceiling catwalk. From the engine room, occasionally I heard the signal bells of the men navigating in the turret.

The pirates were in full control of the Nemo now—of that I had no doubt. The fight was over... I stared up at the catwalk, watching two figures carrying a man between them. He was one of the Nemo's crew; badly wounded so that now he groaned as they carried him. I made out from what I heard that the surviving members of the Nemo's officers and crew were imprisoned in a rear compartment, behind a cross-bulkhead. And now I saw, lying near the engine room arcade, the dead body of one of the oilers, ignored there where he had fallen.

TEN MINUTES or so passed. The submarine was submerged, and proceeding slowly. Across the bunkroom, behind the silent seated figure of my guard, there was a porthole. I could glimpse the turgid blackgreen depths outside. Once a channel sub-surface light went by, but then we turned and apparently left the channel. Heading now for Effinstein's landing stage. I presently saw the ship's cautious, short-range search beam moving back along the hull-side. It gave me a glimpse of the ooze-bottom nearly a fathom or so below us, over which we were slowly passing.

There was another interval. Then a clanging of bells. The hasty tramp of feet. We had arrived at Effinstein's submarine mooring. The distorted shapes of girders were sliding by the port.

A voice said: "Spiggoty! You, Ruffo! The boss says bring that nipper to the turret. We're goin' out in a minute. Gorry, man, you seen the ingots? This is a haul for a lifetime."

The guard jerked me to my feet, shoved me along the side catwalk of the clanging engine room and up the spiral incline to the turret.

The burly ruffian was Pelegrino. Some one called him by name. He and two others were here at the controls, but they barely noticed me. I was flung to a bench, with my guard at my side.

The turret was dark, with only a shaded silver sheen on its instrument dials. Circular convex visor-panes surrounded us, and through them I could see the water outside. Hooded lights were out there on the girders. We were nosing into the slips. The swinging girders came slowly clamping down. I felt us sink into the ooze with a faint jar; the ship's bells rang again; the whirling engines throbbed and stopped.

We had contacted. Outside, on one of the horizontal girders which had a catwalk under it, three grotesque helmeted figures swayed with mooring chains while another held a spreading torchlight. The hooks were jammed into our deck rings. The light swung in an arc for a signal. A distant motordrum tightened the great linked cables to hold us firm.

It was all done so smoothly, swiftly, I could not help a feeling of admiration for these submarine harbor pirates. There was no fumbling; no undue confusion. Through the turret visor Pelegrino was giving his orders; and the man on the dark catwalk answered and relayed them.

In a moment the tube-like landing pressure-port came sliding out from shoreward—a giant telescoping tube some ten feet in diameter and fifty feet long when extended to the full. It slid out from where, ahead of our bow, the network of girders connected with a submerged building. Like a great snake the pressure tube came sliding just above the Nemo's deck. It stopped at the base of our turret where a small exit port projected, and its flexible circular lip made contact there.

The outside, bloated figures leaped to our deck, the tube-end was bolted fast in a moment and one of the figures swung his light when it was done.

"Bueno!" said Pelegrino. "We go ashore, you nipper. Now you see your partner!"

I was with the first batch of men who went into the pressure tube. Pelegrino shoved me now. There were half a dozen other men. Two of them were carrying a small, rough-cast bar of platinum. They staggered with its weight. The first ingot of this whitemetal treasure cargo! The pirates inspected it with triumph.

"When the Jew sees this!"

"You think he'll give our price?"

"Damme, leave that to the boss, eh, Pelegrino?"

"But Effinstein will haf trouble, no? Selling all this, in secret?"

"The hell with that! It ain't our affair, eh, boss? We deliver it here—he does the rest. For us—as the boss says—South America is a healthy place. Eh, boss?"

As we left the Nemo, I heard the distant groans of the wounded and dying crew, imprisoned back of the stern bulkhead.

We were only in the pressurechamber of the tube for a moment. The Nemo's interior air pressure was almost the same as that which Effinstein was maintaining in his subterranean rooms. I was shoved by Pelegrino and the triumphant pirates along the tube's length; into the landing room; down a winding blue-lit corridor.

And at last, with the welcoming shouts of the men—and their triumph at the first of the ingots to be unloaded—making a turmoil of confusion, we reached the familiar lighted room at which I had peered from outside.

Effinstein and his men were here. Josefa was standing against the wall. Dirk, pale and watchful, still sat in the chair with his legs lashed to its lower rungs. He gave me a look of astonished horror as I was dragged forward and flung at his feet.

CHAPTER X

DEATH FOR ALL?

"**BUT, JAC, HOW** in Heaven's name did it happen?" Dirk and I had a moment to exchange whispers.

"I got your hand-message. I took our boat—"

He stared at me silently as I told him. I made no move to rise from where I had been thrown. It seemed that for the moment we were almost ignored. Twenty or thirty men were crowding this and the adjoining room. The platinum ingots were being brought ashore; the place was a confusion of excited voices. I crouched as though in terror at Dirk's feet, whispering to him; and my fingers were fumbling at his legs where they were bound to the chair. It seemed that I might release him.

"Are you armed, Jac?"

"No. They took my gun."

"Mine, too."

"But there must be some way out. Which is the way to the upper exit?"

"I don't know," he murmured. "I've been sitting right here—I've seen nothing."

"If we could make a dash for it—while they're all interested in the treasure. Move your leg! Is it free?"

"Yes—one. Work on the other! Higher up, Jac! Under the knee."

"The girl Josefa is watching us."

"Yes, I see her. She saved my life a while ago—they would have killed me."

"They'll kill us now, right enough, when they get around to thinking of it. Jerk your knee! Is it loose?"

"Yes, I think so."

There seemed no possible way for us to make a dash. The room had two door arcades into other apartments, but both were blocked with the crowding men. We caught snatches of their talk. The Nemo was to be run out and stranded near the main channel. It had carried no passengers. Its officers and crew, imprisoned within the stern bulkhead room, might be found and rescued—or not—as fate decreed. Effinstein and his men would later dispose of the treasure piecemeal through the underworld markets of Great-New York. Pelegrino and the others, paid off now by Effinstein, were about to decamp. And Josefa was going with Pelegrino. We saw him throw his arms about her with a rough, good natured caress.

"Rich, my girl," he said in Spanish. "Is it not as I told you it would be? Riches and the world of the south before us."

TO ONE side of where they were standing I noticed a large circular metal plate fitted into the wall. It was at the floor, some five feet in diameter. A round knob, like a door handle, was at its side; and a foot farther, on the wall, was a lever with a pressure dial over it.

I nudged Dirk to follow my gaze. "What is that? A pressure port?"

"Seems so. A pressure room beyond it. No one has been in or out of it. I was thinking if we could get there with a run— Don't move, Jac! Lie against my legs! Here comes Pelegrino."

With his arm about Josefa's shoulders Pelegrino was advancing. I stared at the pressure port and its dial. The pointer seemed to indicate that the pressure room now was empty of water. If we could get in there—slam that round metal door—hold it against the rush of the pirates… But to escape, we would have to open the outer door and let in the water. And we would need under-water suits. The mechanism was not wholly strange to me. I realized that the lever here was a manual control by which the outer water-port could be opened.

It was an instant rush of thoughts. Pelegrino and Josefa stood before us. The girl avoided our gaze—she was not yet a hardened criminal, and because Dirk had treated her kindly in that Rivington lodging house she could not face him now.

Pelegrino was in high good humor. He leered down at us. "You two nippers—a bad night for you, no?" He chuckled as he met my upturned gaze.

"You tell my men—'God's truth, pirates come to attack the Nemo. Call the Harbor Police!' He do that, Josefa. What you think of that? He mos' earnestly hope we call for the police."

Dirk said abruptly, "What do you propose to do with us?"

"You? A little knife—a little flashbolt—a little water in the lungs. We have many choice, eh, Josefa? The dead man, he do not talk."

"We can't talk," said Dirk. "We don't know any more than the men on the Nemo, for instance. Suppose you put us with them."

"You lie. You know me—Pelegrino. You come to that house where Josefa live. For me, I do not care. I will be gone. But Effinstein—he lay you away in the water."

His gesture sent a shudder over me. Dirk said no more, and I crouched against him to hide where I had freed his legs.

"I see you again," Pelegrino added. "Josefa, come look at the treasure. The white metal to make us rich for always."

They moved away. My breath suddenly stopped. Across the room, that round pressure-port was slowly opening inward! An inch; then another.

"Dirk!"

"I see it."

I could feel Dirk tense. I was ready to spring to my feet. The port swung another inch. No one but us had noticed it. Several men were on the opposite side of the room. Between us and the port there was momentarily no obstruction.

Another inch. Then abruptly, upon silent hinges, it swung wide! One of the pirates let out a startled oath. Dirk and I leaped to our feet. In the circular frame of the opened port, with the dim, air filled pressure chamber behind, stood a figure.

RAMON! HIS pressure-suit was deflated, hanging in folds on his slight frame. The helmet was discarded. His head, with its wavy black hair, pallid face and blazing eyes, seemed grotesquely small above the sagging metal collar.

His voice rang out:

"You stand still! No one move!" And in Spanish:

"If any one moves, it will be death for us all!"

The room was stricken for an instant. No shot came. And in that instant Ramon reached behind him and gripped a lever in the pressure room. He swayed it a trifle, and the one on the wall before us swayed in unison.

"I will let in the water if you move!"

I was aware of Dirk's voice. "Over there—protect him with our bodies from a shot!"

As we leaped, I called, "Ramon! Hold steady!"

One of the pirates shouted something. Some one fired a tiny bolt, but I saw another man knock up the weapon. The bolt hissed against the ceiling with a shower of sparks. The smell of the released gases suffused the room.

We reached Ramon; stood protectingly before him. They could shoot at us. But while they were killing us, he could jerk the lever and open the port. The air would go out in a gulp, like a giant under water, exhaling; and with a pressure of many tons the water would surge in. Nothing could check it, once the flood came. It would be death to every one here in these subterranean rooms.

Again there was a moment of horrified inactivity. Then a clatter. Men running in from the back rooms to see what had happened; standing stricken with confusion and horror in the doorways; low curses; a shout from Pelegrino; Effinstein shouting with a quaver:

"You couldn't do that! Let it alone! You will kill us all!"

And mingled with it, a scream from Josefa. "Ramon! Ramon!"

"Josefa! Come here—"

I was murmuring to Dirk, "Can we get back in there? Close this port?"

"No suits! Ramon, are there any suits?"

"No! I saw none! Josefa, come here!"

For an instant she seemed undecided. Then she jerked from Pelegrino and came running. I shoved her behind us; Ramon seized her and pushed her back into the pressure room.

Pelegrino was shouting:

"You fools! Come from that! You will kill us all!"

Then Dirk took a hand. "Get back, all of you! Over there against the wall! If any one fires—or even moves toward us—we'll open the port! What is death to us? You'll kill us anyway."

I SAW Pelegrino's gaze alertly roving the room, trying to figure what he might do. He was standing in advance of his confused comrades. His small electronic gun was in his hand, but he did not dare level it.

"Maybe we not kill you," he offered. "You say you want that I put you on the Nemo. Come from that port—"

"Not yet," said Dirk.

Both of them were stalling, wondering what they could do. Behind me, Ramon was whispering:

"*Señor,* there is no escape. We have but this one suit. Cannot I give it to Josefa? We stand in the other room—then she get away, into the water—"

"Ramon! No!" She was clinging to him now.

"You!" shouted Dirk. "You Effinstein?"

Effinstein was close behind Pelegrino. He had a gun in his hand, and he seemed to be raising it very slowly.

I shouted, "Put down that gun! Drop it, I tell you!"

The gun clattered to the floor. I felt Dirk suddenly clutching me. And he whispered, "Jac! Hear that outside? And overhead? Make a noise! Talk fast!"

And Dirk began vehemently shouting:

"You'll have to bring us pressure suits! You, Pelegrino—you Effinstein! Get us pressure suits!"

And my loud voice joined with his: "Pressure suits! Give us pressure suits! Let us out of here or we'll kill you! Let us out—"

We made all the noise we could. And over it I tried to strain my ears. There were noises outside, and in the distance overhead. Muffled thuds… I thought I heard running footsteps. Then across the room, where the round bull's-eye pane showed a vista of the outer water, I saw, out there in the water—a flash! And another! The Nemo was being attacked! There was fighting outside! And overhead—running footsteps. They were suddenly plain to hear. The sound of a shot, inside the upper passages of this subterranean labyrinth!

Dirk's voice and mine could only hide it for an instant. Men in the adjoining room were shouting. Then running. There was an exchange of shots quite near at hand.

"Back out of here!" Dirk suddenly shouted. "We won't open the port. Run—if you think you can get away!"

The men behind Pelegrino and Effinstein were edging back, and abruptly they turned and ran. But a shot in the adjoining room greeted them. Pelegrino took a step forward. I thought for an instant that he would blindly fire upon us. But instead he leaped for the door oval near by.

Dirk was shoving me back. "Get this pressure-port closed! Get behind it! This attack will be over in a minute!"

The fighting was already here. I saw Effinstein turn to run, but from the next room a bolt darted. It caught him full and he went down upon his face with arms flung over his head.

Electronic weapons, discharged indoors, are unutterably horrible. The place was a mad turmoil of confusion now. The hiss of the bolts, thuds of falling bodies, oaths and screams and heavy pounding footsteps echoed from everywhere. Turgid gas fumes were surging in upon us.

We were unarmed. Any stray shot from the attackers, or from the fast yielding pirates caught down here like rats in a trap, could have killed us. Dirk swung the pressure port shield close upon us. In the darkness we crouched, listening to the sounds of the struggle.

BESIDE ME, Josefa was clinging to Ramon. I heard him telling her how he had been able to come through this outer port into the water-filled pressure-chamber; had fumbled with the controls, by chance finding at last how to empty it of the water; and in the confusion of the Nemo's arrival the dim sound of its pumps had passed unnoticed.

"It's over, Jac." Dirk was peering through the crack of our partly opened port. Then he swung it wide.

My call for help from the little boat as I headed for the Nemo had gotten through. This was the Harbor Police. We confronted one of the captains.

"You—Franklin Dirk? Good Lord, I wondered where you were. This fellow here—he seems to be the leader—" the captain was saying.

A group of the police were crowding the room, with the burly Pelegrino among them. He stumbled upon the dead body of Effinstein as they shoved him forward. Suddenly he stooped. Effinstein's small flash-gun still lay there unnoticed. And Pelegrino seized it. Raised it, all in a second, and screamed:

"You bring this upon me!"

It was Josefa at whom he leaped. The movement was so unexpected it caught every one unaware. The girl was quite near him. He must have pressed the trigger of the gun. I heard its sharp click, but the loads were exhausted. Or it was out of order. Then, with his leap, he whirled it to crash it upon Josefa's head.

We were all so close together that none of the police dared fire. I tried to jump for Pelegrino, but Ramon was ahead of me.

His knife came down. Pelegrino sank backward and lay with the knife handle sticking like a little implanted cross on his chest.

"I have done it! At last it is done!" I think I have never seen such grim triumph as the pale, blazing eyes Ramon flung about the room.

"My sister—she is only sixteen, and he take her from me." He babbled it in English, in explanation to us all. "She is so young—she think she love him. Josefa, that is over now. Little sister, you stay always with Ramon."

Himself almost as young as she, he stood holding her protectingly in his arms, as though never again would he let her go.

ABOUT THE AUTHOR

"**HE IS A** Verne returned and Wells going forward," remarked "Bob" Davis, dean of American magazine editors. "He is the American H.G. Wells," say other critics.

Cummings has an unusual flair for things scientific as evidenced by the fact that while at Princeton University he accomplished the remarkable feat of absorbing three years of physics in that many months. His five years' association with Thomas A. Edison as the latter's personal assistant also added to Cummings's scientific knowledge. His bizarre early life, living on orange plantations in Puerto Rico, striking oil in Wyoming, gold seeking in British Columbia, timber cruising in the North, before he was twenty, also left its imprint.

Leaving Mr. Edison's employ, Cummings began writing scientific fiction for many magazines. His stories gripped the popular imagination and they "clicked." Mr. Cummings's success as a writer has been meteoric, for in a few years he has become one of the world's most popular authors of scientific fiction.

Yet when asked about his own life and experiences Mr. Cummings is shy and evasive. He would much rather talk about Miss Betty Starr Cummings, his four-year-old daughter, whom he terms "the really interesting member of the family."

A few of her exploits include being wrecked and transshipped in a heavy sea; adrift with her parents in a disabled open boat when only three weeks old; traveling thousands of miles by automobile, train and steamer; weathering a Florida hurricane and coming safely through an automobile accident. From all of which we can see that Mr. Cummings leads rather an adventurous life himself!

Ray Cummings

Winter finds him at home in Bermuda, but when the temperature starts to rise he quickly makes tracks for Quebec. As we write this a letter arrives from Bermuda announcing that his next full length fantastic novel will soon be ready for *Argosy* readers.

In the office of *Fantastic Novels* the other day, Mr. Cummings looked this autobiography over with a smile. "It's all right," he said, "except that Betty is fourteen and has already sold a story of her own, which she wrote when she was thirteen. Fulton Oursler accepted it for *Liberty Magazine!*"

Asked about how he came to write "The Girl in the Golden Atom," Mr. Cummings said that it was the very first thing that he ever wrote, and that he did it simply because he felt like putting down and developing the idea of entering a world inside a ring. He had no thought of selling it, nor even that it might be a usable story. Two friends, William C. McNulty, an important American etcher, and Spring Byington, motion picture actress (known nowadays as *the mother* in "The Jones Family" on the radio) looked over the story, and liked it. Mr. Cummings, who knew no rules for writing but simply put it down "straight from the heart" read it aloud to Mr. McNulty and to Miss Byington when either of them asked how it was coming along. They were very enthusiastic and urged him to take it to a publisher. Bob Davis snapped it up.

And Ray Cummings has been writing ever since.

www.ingramcontent.com/pod-product-compliance
Lightning Source LLC
LaVergne TN
LVHW090959080826
845145LV00003B/1057
9781618276360